Christ-Consciousness

Sebastian Painadath SJ

Sr. Rose Pudukadan

Christ-Consciousness

Contemplation with *Jesus Prayer*

2018

Christ-Consciousness: Contemplation with *Jesus Prayer* — published by the Rev. Dr. Ashish Amos of the Indian Society for Promoting Christian Knowledge (ISPCK), Post Box 1585, 1654, Madarsa Road, Kashmere Gate, Delhi-110006.

Online Order: http://ispck.org.in/book.php

Also available on amazon

ISBN: 978-81-8465-683-1

Cover design: Darshana, Kalady

Laser typeset by

ISPCK, Post Box 1585, 1654, Madarsa Road, Kashmere Gate, Delhi-110006
Tel: 23866323

e-mail: ashish@ispck.org.in • ella@ispck.org.in
website: www.ispck.org.in

Contents

Preface

The *Prayer of the Name* is a popular form found practically in all religions. One goes on repeating the name of the divine Lord that one regards as sacred. The divine name contains enormous spiritual energies. By constant devotional repetition these energies are released and the spiritual aspirant is taken to deeper levels of consciousness. Though it is a form of popular devotion, it is in fact a contemplative way to experience the divine presence. It is simple, effective, accessible to all at any time of the day. It is a way of elevating oneself to the awareness of the Divine in the midst of daily engagements.

This prayer form is also called the *Prayer of the heart*. Through the repetition of the divine name consciousness sinks from the mind to the heart, the core of the person. *Heart* is a symbol found in all religions to designate the sacred space within us. It is in the heart that one sinks into a mystical union. Within the heart there is no duality, no I-thou-polarity. Here one sinks into a deep contemplative silence. The experience of the divine presence is a grace felt in the heart; one may reflect on this at the mind level and articulate in words of vocal prayer.

In Christian tradition this prayer form is called *Jesus Prayer*. The name that conveys the experience of the Divine for Christians is Jesus. Hence we Christians go on repeating the name of Jesus in an attitude of self-surrender. Gradually awareness sinks from verbal repetition to a receptive mood of interior silence. Within the heart one experiences Christ-consciousness: one's being *in Christ*.

Jesus Prayer is also *Prayer in the Spirit*. The divine Spirit carves deeper and leads one to the "depths of God". From an object-related vocal prayer one is taken to the experience of the Divine as subject. The God to whom we pray, is the God who prays within us "in a way that cannot be put into words." God-as-Spirit is the true subject of prayer. The soul merges with the divine Spirit: they become ONE. The realisation that *I am divine* is the most sublime grace of contemplation, the deepest meeting point of all religions.

This book is born of praxis. Over several years we have been conducting meditation courses in India and abroad initiating spiritual sadhakas to Jesus Prayer. This experience together with the feed-back of the participants encouraged us to present this theme in a book form for wider reception. The book contains theological reflections as well as concrete methods for practising Jesus Prayer. A specific contribution of this book is that it offers forms of Jesus Prayer with mantras taken from the spiritual heritage of India. When the name of Jesus is chanted with a divine mantra like OM, the spiritual energies immanent in the name unfold and consciousness sinks into the spiritual heart. Mantra is a powerful means in the transition from vocal prayer to contemplation. By chanting the name of Jesus with a mantra one gets deepened in Christ-consciousness.

The dominant prayer forms supported by the Catholic Charismatic Movement have become very noisy. Those who have grown in it now look for ways to interior silence. Jesus Prayer is a contemplative form with a Christo-centric spirituality. As one grows in the practice of Jesus Prayer one is led by the Spirit from a devotional surrender to the divine person of Jesus (*bhakti*) to a contemplative experience of the indwelling Christ (*jnana*). Empowered by this experience one gets engaged in the world (*karma*) as channel of the Spirit in bringing about a new creation.

The chapters of this book are arranged in four parts:

I. After a survey of the practice of praying the name in world religions (ch.1) the historical evolution of Jesus Prayer is described (ch.2). Then we look into the levels of the introspective journey (ch.3) to have clarity on the process through prayer, meditation and contemplation (ch. 4).

II. In the second part we explore the dimensions of Christ-consciousness as described in the Gospel of John (ch.5) and try to grasp the significance of the divinisation of the human as understood by the Church Fathers (ch.6). On this background we reflect on the spirituality (ch. 7) and theology of Jesus Prayer (ch. 8).

III. In the third part we take note of the Scriptural passages referring to the name of Jesus (ch.9) and then examine some of the mystical characteristics of Jesus Prayer (ch.10) and its fruits (ch.11).

IV. The fourth part takes us to the concrete practice of Jesus Prayer. Some ways of practising Jesus Prayer are first indicated (ch.12). Then (ch.13) fifteen meditations with Jesus Prayer are proposed. Every meditation is introduced with an appropriate story and a short reflection on the theme; some pertinent quotations from classical sources are offered by way of inspiration. The first three meditations related to earth, body and breath are simple helps to get into interior silence. For the other meditations certain mantra-forms are proposed; however each one should use the freedom to choose an invocation form that resonates with oneself. It may be better to practise one or the other meditation for a longer period, till one experiences the inherent vibrations evoked by the chanting of the name of Jesus. The overall fruit of these meditations is the deepening of Christ-consciousness by the practice of Jesus Prayer.

Gratefully we remember the hundreds of participants who took meditation courses with us: we are thankful to them for their keen interest and positive feedback, which contributed much to the composition of this book. A special gratitude to Fr. Dr. George Nedungatt SJ, an expert in the spirituality of the Eastern Churches, for carefully reading the manuscript and for his valuable suggestions. We thank ISPCK, Delhi, for publishing this book. Much of the content of this book has been published in the German book: Sebastian Painadath SJ / Rose Pudukadan, *Das Herz in Schwingung bringen, Jesus-Gebet mit Mantras und Melodien*, Vier-Türme-Verlag, Münsterschwarzach, 2014.

It is our hope that these reflections and meditations would help many spiritual seekers to deepen their spirituality with the practice of Jesus Prayer.

08 September 2018

Sebastian Painadath SJ
spainadath@gmail.com

Sr. Rose Pudukadan
srrosepd@gmail.com

1
Prayer of the Name in World Religions

We live in a new phase of the spiritual evolution of humanity. The international travel facilities and intercontinental communication media have created a global consciousness, that as human beings we form one global family. In this process religions too play a unifying role, though at times they let loose divisive forces. A deep sense of the mystery of the Divine, a genuine concern for the integral welfare of the human and an effective commitment to the protection of environment are the common concerns of all religions. With these, a global spirituality, within and beyond world religions, evolves in the hearts of the seekers everywhere. An intense quest for the mystical experience of the Divine is a characteristic of the present world. We need to respect the diversity of religious beliefs, and we have to explore the unity in a humanising spirituality.

Prayer of the Name in Hinduism

All Hindu traditions encourage this form of prayer in its simplicity and power. There are three classical traditions of Hinduism related to Siva, Vishnu and the Mother Goddess Sakti. Those who worship Siva chant *OM namah Sivāya*. Those who invoke Vishnu chant *OM namō Nārāya-nāya*. In Śakti cult they repeat *OM Śakti..OM Śakti..OM Śakti OM....*, by which the power of the divine Mother is invoked. In most Indian traditions the name of the Lord is chanted with the mantra OM, which is the sound symbol of the Divine. The chanting of the name of the Lord with the mantra OM creates enormous spiritual vibrations in the cave of the heart, the sacred space within.

Prayer of the Name in Buddhism

In classical Buddhism Buddha is never invoked as a deity. Yet the name of Buddha is sacred for Buddhists to reach nirvana. Hence in the course of time a devotional repetition of the name of Buddha became a popular practice. The classical formula is

Buddham śaranam gacchāmi, (I take refuge in the Buddha.)

Dhammam śaranam gacchāmi, (I take refuge in the Dharma, righteousness)

Samgham śaranam gacchāmi. (I take refuge in the community)

In local traditions other forms developed like:

OM *mani padmē hum* (the pearl in the lotus of the heart) or

Namō amita butsu. (I pay homage to Amita Buddha).

With these words devotees are not worshipping Buddha, but waking to the Buddha consciousness.

Prayer of the Name in Islam

The most sacred name for God in Islam is Allah. Other 99 names of God are also found in the Quran. Muslim devotees practise the repetition of these 99 names using beads. The Sufis, the mystics of Islam, have practised and popularised the prayer of the name as an effective means for the realisation of oneness with God.

Prayer of the Name in Sikhism

Sikkhism is a religion that evolved in the 15th century in India through a spiritual encounter between Islam and Hinduism. The devotional chanting of the name of God is basic to the Sikh religious practice. In the Adi Granth, Guru Nanak (1466-1539) exhorts the believers: "Let us repeat God´s name. As he was in the beginning the Truth, so is he now the Truth, so will he be forever and ever." (1,1)

Great sages and saints of all religions have attained a deep mystical experience of union with the Divine through the constant practice of a meditative repetition of the name of the divine Lord. Mahatma Gandhi calls this simple form of prayer "the poor man´s medicine". He breathed his last by repeating the name of the Lord: *hē Ram...* (Ram refers to the all pervading presence of the Divine in the universe).

The Historical Evolution of Jesus Prayer

Jesus Prayer, or the *Prayer of the Name,* is a form of prayer that belongs to the Christian mystical heritage. One repeats the name of Jesus Christ in an attitude of genuine self-surrender. But while repeating the name of Jesus one finds oneself in the mystical stream of the spiritual seekers of all religions. Jesus Prayer inserts us deeper to the spiritual heritage of humanity. "We call God by many names, without however completely exhausting the divine reality, which is beyond us" (John Paul II, Senegal, 20.02.1992). With the followers of other religions we are spiritual *co-pilgrims.*[1]

What is the specific contribution of the Christian faith for a liberative global spirituality? This is not just a matter of theological clarity, but an invitation to lived praxis. The divine mystery reveals itself in diverse ways. We Christians have experienced in Jesus Christ the embodied self-giving of the Divine in history. If the person and event of Jesus the Christ is the core of Christian faith, we need to seek ways and means to experience the mystical reality of Christ and live out the liberative message of Jesus. Though it is through the historical Jesus that we experience God´s self-revelation, the focus of our faith is the reality of Christ in the present. As Paul and John make it clear, we live and move and have our being *in Christ.* Christ is the presence of the Divine within and all around us. A revitalisation of this mystical dimension of the Christian faith is an epochal need today.

It is with this in view that we turn to the practice of Jesus Prayer. Jesus Prayer is a simple, but effective means of revitalising the mystical dimension in our Christian faith experience. Jesus Prayer is regarded as the contemplative prayer *par excellence.* It is highly christocentric. Through the practice of Jesus Prayer we are not worshipping Jesus who lived two thousand years ago, but we are waking our consciousness to the power and presence of the Divine in the present, to the reality of the risen Christ here and now.

There are five factors which make the praxis of Jesus Prayer effective and powerful:

1. Jesus Prayer is a classical form of mystical prayer in the Christian tradition. From the time of Desert Fathers, who lived in the Egyptian Desert during the 4th and 5th centuries, the prayer of the name of Jesus was practised in Christian circles. It received wider acceptance in the Greek Eastern Churches across the centuries. Now it is spreading to the West as well.

2. The essence of Jesus Prayer is that it is an inner spiritual prayer: the attention is focused on the indwelling presence of Christ in the *heart*. The vocal repetition of the divine name of Jesus is a preparation for the inner spiritual prayer. Jesus Prayer is accessible to any spiritual seeker at any moment of daily life. Through a disciplined practice the name of the Lord gets grafted into the heart and one comes to the realisation that the divine name repeats itself even without one´s being aware of it.

3. Jesus Prayer takes us to the very heart of Christian God-experience. Consciousness sinks from the upper levels of the mind to the depths of the heart. And in the heart we experience a deep communion with Christ-in-us, a deep mystical oneness in the Divine. Here we realise what Jesus meant with the words: "The glory that you have given me I have given them, so that they may be one, as we are one" (Jn. 17:22). We realise that our life evolves not before God, but within the Divine, within the inner-Trinitarian life. The ultimate goal of Jesus Prayer is the attainment of Christ-consciousness.

4. Jesus Prayer can be a healing experience in our psychic life. On our inward spiritual journey we pass through the jungle of the psyche, where a lot of suppressed emotions and wounded feelings constantly disturb us. The spiritual masters recommend the practice of Jesus

Prayer as a torch-light to find our way through this psychic jungle. A deep inner healing can take place in us.

5. The meditative repetition of the name of the divine Lord is a common practice found in several world religions. Jesus Prayer belongs to this common spiritual patrimony of religions. The conviction that the name of the Lord contains divine energy is behind this universal practice. Through the repetition of the name the divine energy contained in the name deepens our consciousness. In most religious traditions people use the beads for this prayer form.

There are three phases in the historical evolution of the practice of Jesus Prayer. [2]

First Phase: In Sinai

The practice of Jesus prayer began with the Desert Fathers. They lived in the Egyptian desert in 4-5 centuries. With the declaration of Christianity as the imperial religion the period of persecution and martyrdom came to an end. However a heroic surrendering of one's life for Christ was considered to be a high ideal. With this aim in mind some went to the Egyptian desert and lived a life of radical renunciation and prayer. In order to face the struggles of austere life in the desert and to conquer the onslaught of loneliness they started to invoke the name of Jesus. They practised the simple form of prayer by repeating just the name: JESUS. This method was called Monologia (*monos*= one, *logos* = word). This was the beginning of the spiritual heritage of Jesus Prayer. "The brethren in Egypt offer prayers that are frequent, but very brief, and suddenly shot forth." (Augustine, PL.33, 501)[3]

Their purpose was to remain in the constant awareness of the presence of God. For this they found in the devotional repetition of the name of Jesus an effective help. With this they could relish an outer and inner silence. They lived in spiritual happiness coming out of the abiding sense of the presence of God within and all around them. They lived in the experience of God´s love, inner joy and peace.

This primal form was called Hesychia. It is a Greek word meaning quietness, stillness, tranquillity. Mind goes deep into inner silence. A mystical experience of the soul being one with the divine Spirit emerges. This is the experience of deep mystical union. There is only the sense of the presence of the Divine within. The divine Spirit fully takes hold of the human soul. Gregory of Nyssa says: "Hesychia is a pure prayer free from images and concepts".[4] This alertness is called *nipsis* (sobriety), which is one of the main characteristics of Jesus Prayer.

For the Desert Fathers Jesus Prayer was not just a matter of exercise; it was rather an integral way of life. They practiced it not only in their prayer times, but also throughout the day and night. They lived in genuine asceticism, spiritual discipline and availability to seekers, who came for spiritual guidance; they were called spiritual masters (*homines spirituales*).

Evagrios Pontikos (345-399) has been a major spiritual master of this tradition. Evagrios insisted that in meditation one should go beyond all images and forms in pursuit of deep God-experience. Images and forms can be helpful only at the initial stage. But as one goes deeper into silence they vanish. A sense of inner void is then felt. In this void one just sits in the experience of the presence of the Divine. When all images and forms vanish, only the name of JESUS lingers on. One sits concentrated on his inner presence by repeating the name of Jesus. As consciousness further sinks even the name disappears. One enters into a deep sense of spiritual contemplative silence of the presence of God. Evagrios integrated the Monologia practice of the Desert Fathers with the theological insights of Origen of Alexandria. This was his great theological and spiritual contribution. His major writings are *Problemata Gnostika* with 600 verses, and *Antirrhetikos* in eight books.

There were Buddhist *samghas* (communities) in the Northern Nile valley since 250. BC. Initially they were sent by Aśoka (274-232 BC) from India with the mission to spread the message of non-violence, spiritual discipline and herbal wisdom. These sages practiced severe asceticism and deep meditation. Buddhist monks had the practice of repeating the name of Buddha to get into the deeper levels of consciousness in order to realise the Buddha-nature. This may have had some indirect influence on the emergence of the practice of Jesus Prayer in Christian circles.[5]

St. Diadochos, bishop of Photike (-458), in his *Hundred Chapters on Perfection* 59, recommends purifying the heart through the remembrance of Jesus. "We ought to give to the *nous* nothing but the words *Lord Jesus!*"[6]

St. Hesychius (-450) is one of the spiritual masters mentioned in *The Centuries*, a 15th century classic on Jesus-Prayer. He speaks of repeating the name of Jesus with the rhythm of breathing. "May the remembrance of Jesus be united to your breathing and to your whole life" (*The Centuries, I.99*). "The name of Jesus appears first of all as a lamp in the darkness, next like the moonlight and finally like a sunrise" (*The Centuries, II.64*). "Being the sun of our *nous* it creates within luminous thoughts to which it communicates its own splendour, thoughts resembling the sun" (*The Centuries, II. 94*).

Barsanuphius and John the Prophet (-540) in their *840 Spiritual Letters* recommend abandonment of one´s own will, spiritual direction, examination of conscience and the invocation of the name of Jesus. For the beginners in spiritual life they recommend the practice of Jesus Prayer to confront temptations and struggles.

John Klimakos (580-649) in his spiritual classic *The Ladder of Divine Ascent* describes how interior prayer goes into deeper levels of God-awareness. He proposes that the name of Jesus could be repeated with the breathing. This helps to attain concentration. John Klimakos describes the process of prayer as a movement from discursive thought (*logismoi*) to introspection through just one word (*monologia*). The "eye of the heart" is illuminated to see the "divine Sun of the intelligence" and the soul is fully luminous. "May the remembrance of Jesus be united to your breathing and then you will know the value of hesychia" (*Ladder, 27. PG. 88. 1112C*).

Symeon the new Theologian (949-1022) was the last master of the Hesychia tradition. He insisted on the primacy of contemplation over intellectual and active life, the primacy of the pneumatic element over the hierarchical structure. Symeon had an enlightenment experience while reciting Jesus Prayer. He felt himself entirely light-filled. He experienced light, sweetness and tears. He had a vision of the Logos made flesh in Jesus, the luminous form of the Divine. The spiritual Classic, *Method of Holy Prayer and Attention* is attributed to Symeon. (PG. 120, 701-710). He describes Jesus Prayer as a way to experience the "epiclesis of Christ"

The term "Jesus Prayer" (*euche tou Jesou*) is first used in the classic *The Centuries*. It also uses the expression *epiclesis Jesou* =the coming down of Jesus.[7]

Second Phase: On Mount Athos

In the 14th century a large number of monks lived in Athos. Their main form of prayer was Jesus Prayer.

Gregory of Sinai (1255-1346) was a monk in Cypress. Later he spent some time in Sinai. He met the ascetic Arsenius in Crete. Thus he was introduced to the hesychasm tradition of Sinai. He later got settled as monk on Mt. Athos. It was through him that the practice of Jesus Prayer entered Athos. He is recognised as the Teacher of Holy Sobriety, guarding of the heart. Later in 1325 he established a monastery on Mount Paroria near the Black Sea in order to promote the practice of Jesus Prayer. He describes the theological foundations of mystical life in terms of *energia*, an active manifestation and operation of the Spirit, which is latent in us; this can be activated in two ways: the way of the commandments and the way of the continual invocation of the name of Jesus, by which the *nous* is immersed into the heart. The soul is thus nourished by the divine name as the body is nourished by food. He also advises to stick to one formula of repeating the name. At Athos the formula practised was "Jesus Christ Son of God, have mercy on me". At Sinai till then other variants were allowed. As a result the spontaneity and tenderness which marked the Sinai tradition was partly lost on Athos. He wrote the books: *137 Chapters on Spiritual Meditations*, with aphorisms of the Desert Fathers, *On Stillness and Prayer* (PG 150,1304-12), *The Two Methods of Prayer* (PG 150.1313-29) and *How a Hesychast should sit for Prayer* (PG. 150.1329-45).

Theoleptus, monk on Athos, later made Archbishop of Philadelphia (-1320) was the revered master of Gregory Palamas. He says: "Pure prayer reunites in itself the nous, the Logos (Word) and the Pneuma (Spirit). Through the Logos it invokes God´s name. Through the nous it calmly fixes its gaze on the God whom it invokes. Through the Pneuma (Spirit) it manifests compunction, humility and love. In this way it calls upon the eternal Trinity the one and only God" (PG 143. 393BC).

St. Gregory of Palamas (1296-1360) was a monk of Athos, later Archbishop of Thessaloniki. He spoke of the divine *essence* as the unfathomable mystery and imparticipable reality; from this divine source emanate the divine *energies* which transform our life into divine life.[8] Through Jesus Prayer we tune ourselves to the divine energy stream. Jesus Prayer initiates us to the energy field of divine light. Gradually we are blessed with the vision of the divine light in us and outside: *theognosia*.[9] This is participation in the *taboric light* that surrounded Jesus at the Transfiguration on the Mount. For Gregory this is the spiritual goal of hesychasm and of Jesus Prayer. St. Paul experienced this inflow of the divine light when he narrates his experience of ´being caught up into the third heaven´ (II Cor. 12:2-4). "Paul saw a light without limits below or above or to the sides. It was like a sun infinitely brighter and vaster than the universe, and in the midst of this sun he himself stood. Such is the vision of glory to which we may approach through the invocation of the Name. Jesus Prayer causes the brightness of the Transfiguration to penetrate into every corner of our life." (*Triads in Defence of the Holy Hesychasts.*) This is participation in the uncreated energy of the Divine. Gregory consistently makes a distinction between the divine essence, which is beyond our grasp, and the divine energies, in which we participate. He had heated polemics with Barlaam on this. Barlaam insisted on mental prayer and action, while Gregory emphasised Jesus Prayer leading to contemplation and union. Gregory was imprisoned and excommunicated, but later made Archbishop of Thessalonica. The Athos monks supported his teachings. In 1368 his doctrine was declared the official teaching of the Byzantine Church. Gregory is considered to be the spiritual master of the divinisation of the human (*theosis*) in the Greek Eastern Church. Some of the writings of Gregory of Palamas are: *Triads in Defence of the Holy Hesychasts, Three Chapters on Prayer and Purity of Heart, On the Passions and Virtues, Decalogue of the Law According to Christ.*

Nikephoros was a monk of Athos in the 14th century. The classic, *Guardian of the Heart*, is attributed to him. He proposes to repeat the Name with the breath to facilitate the nous enter the heart. "Take away all discursive thought from the reason and give to it the invocation Lord Jesus Christ, Son of God, have mercy on me", and force yourself in place of all other thoughts, always to cry out this prayer within yourself" (PG.147,965-966). He teaches that we are to call to mind Jesus Christ until "the name of the Lord penetrates our heart, descends to its very depths, crushes the dragon and gives life to the soul." Our heart is to absorb the Lord, and the Lord to absorb our heart, and the two are to become one. The name of Jesus, once it has become the centre of our life, brings everything together in harmony. Nikephoros named it the `Prayer of the Presence´. One lives in an abiding sense of the presence of God.

St. Maximos of Kapsokalyvia (14th cent.), an anchorite on Athos, loved solitude so much that he several times burnt his hut to escape the flow of visitors. He prayed ardently to Virgin Mary for the grace of Jesus Prayer. He harmonised Jesus Prayer with devotion to Mary, the Mother of God. He shows how Marian devotion can deepen Christ-consciousness within the heart.

Kallistos and Ignatious Xanthopoulos. (14-15 cent.) were monks on Athos. They composed *The Century, the Hundred Aphorisms*. This book is a complete rule of life for Hesychasts. It gives practical guidelines for this form of prayer: keep the head slightly bent forward, eyes fixed on a point in the heart, bring attention to the core of the heart. In the practice there is a two-fold movement: a soaring ascent towards Jesus Christ in the first part (with in-breath one repeats "Lord Jesus Christ, Son of God"), and a return to oneself in the second part (with the out-breath one repeats "have mercy on me"). This exercise helps to attain concentration. In Hesychia there is no place for quietism. Ascetical practices and vegetarian food are demanded. The goal of Jesus Prayer is an affective merging into Christ, wherein one could say, "I am wounded with love" (Song of Songs, 5:8).

Gradually Athos became the spiritual source and orientation centre of the growth of Jesus Prayer. Monks and spiritual seekers came here from many places, got initiated to this hesychast form of prayer. They then spread this form in Slavic and Byzantine regions. In many places this reached also the common people. Since the Middle Ages the Byzantine monks have associated the recitation of Jesus Prayer with the use of a rosary or prayer-rope, which helps in counting the invocations. The Greek rosary has 100 beads, and the Russian rosary has 107 beads; a rosary was given to the monks and nuns on the day of their monastic profession. To some extent Jesus Prayer formed part of the canonical prayer of the monastic community (*Nomocanon, 87*): the rosary is to be said five times a day. In the practice of Jesus Prayer certain bodily postures were also recommended. There are basically two postures (*metanoia*): one stands and bows deep without bending the knees (*lesser metanoia*), and one kneels and bows forward in full prostration with the forehead touching the ground (*greater metanoia*). But these postures are not essential to the contemplative practice of Jesus Prayer. What is important is the inner attitude of surrender.

Third Phase: In Russia

Some sages who had got initiated to Jesus Prayer on Athos tried to spread this form of contemplative prayer in the Slavic and Russian regions.

St. Nil Sorskij (1433-1508) is a Russian monk who spent several years on Athos, practiced Jesus Prayer and brought it to several parts of the Russian Church. In North Russia a monastic community called Monastery of the Trinity near Obnora (1389) had evolved with the practice of Jesus Prayer. They wanted to live in the heritage of the Hesychia tradition of Sinai. But in the politicised Church context of Russia this monastic venture had no success. The monks were ignored by the Church leadership. Yet Jesus Prayer never disappeared from Russian monasticism, which served as critique on the institutionalism which prevailed in the Russian Church. In the 16th century Jesus Prayer got well established in Russia.

St Dimitri, Metropolitan of Rostov (1651-1709) promoted Jesus Prayer in Russia. His books are: *The Spiritual Medicine* on freeing oneself from evil thoughts and *The Interior Man* on the effectiveness of prayer.

St. Makarios, Metropolitan of Corinth (1731-1805) and Nikodemos Hagiorit (1748-1809) collected the teachings of the ancient Fathers on Jesus Prayer and compiled the *Philokalia* (= Love of the good and the beautiful). This gradually became a classical source book of the theology and practice of Jesus Prayer. The first edition appeared in 1782. This book contains the sayings and teachings of 30 spiritual masters who in the period of 4-14 centuries taught about spiritual life in terms of practising Jesus Prayer. In every aphorism one can feel the power and depth of mystical experience. Be united with

Christ in your heart, deepen the Christic consciousness – this is the experience that the book leads to. Philokalia is a compilation of the teachings on the ways a spiritual seeker should take in pursuit of total self-dedication to and union with God. It deals with: 1. the aim of Christian life, 2. the ways to attain this aim, 3. the impediments which come up on the way, 4. the means to overcome them, 5. the joy in having the mystical vision of the Divine (the spiritual bliss). Philokalia was originally composed in Greek language. Soon it was translated into Russian. In subsequent years it got translated into several other languages. Through Philokalia Jesus Prayer spread to the laity especially in Russia and Greece. Nikodemos Hagiorit in his book *The Manual of Counsel on the Guarding of the Five Senses, the Intellect and the Heart* (1801) insists that it is important to avoid all imaginations and any impression of a form in Jesus Prayer. He quotes Evagrios: "Approach the Immaterial in an immaterial way."[10]

(A new 5 volume set of *Philokalia* with translations in English and Malayalam has been made available by: Dr. Cheriyan Eapen, Roy International Children´s Foundation, 5 b, Century Towers, Kottayam, Kerala, India, 2009)

Passij Velickowskij (1722-1794) lived for some time on Athos and later brought the *Philokalia* to the Slavic people. This Russian seeker compiled in 1793 the teachings of the Slavic and Russian monks on Jesus Prayer in his Russian book *Dobrotolubie* (Love of the Goodness). It contains selected parts of the Philokalia. With this translation even the simple village people became familiar with Jesus Prayer.

(In English: by E. Kadloubovsky and G.E.H. Palmer, *Writings from the Philokalia*, Faber and Faber, paperback edition, NY, 1995.)

(In Malayalam: by Swami Siddhinādhānanada, *Adhyātma Prēmam*, Kurisumala, Vagamon, Kerala, India, 1983)

St. Seraphim of Sarov (1759-1833) is the most popular and mystical saint of Russia. He said: "In order to receive and feel Christ´s light in the heart one must withdraw as much as possible from all visible things. When the soul with inner faith in the Crucified has purified itself by repentance and good works one must close the eyes of the body, make the understanding descend into the heart, and call unceasingly upon the name of our Lord Jesus Christ: *Jesus Christ, Son of God, have mercy on me.* Then a person according to the measure of his zeal and fervour towards the beloved finds in the invocation of the Name consolation and sweetness, and this arouses in him the desire to seek higher illumination."[11]

Ignatius Brianchaninov (1807-1867), Bishop of Kostroma, wrote the book *On the Prayer of Jesus,* in which he recommends this form of prayer to all the faithful.

Theophan the Recluse (1815-1894), Bishop of Tambov, compiled an enlarged edition of the book *Dobrotolubie* with the mystical prayer traditions of the Russian Church. Some of his writings are available in English translation in the book: *The Art of Prayer, An Orthodox Anthology,* (1936/1996) by Igumen Chariton of Valamo. He makes a sharp distinction between the interior Jesus Prayer and the exterior postures, which do not contribute anything essential to the practice. "The union of nous with the heart is a gift of grace. The essence of the practice of Jesus Prayer consists in acquiring the habit of keeping the nous on guard within the heart" (*Dobrotolubie, Moscow, 1889, V. 470*).

The Way of a Pilgrim, (1851-1861). This small book, written by a simple spiritual seeker in Russia between 1855 and 1861 has been instrumental in making Jesus Prayer reach the common people. Its original Russian title meant: *Sincere Tales of a Pilgrim to his Spiritual Father* (Kazan, 1881). It shows vividly how through the practice of Jesus Prayer the pilgrim attained an abiding sense of the presence of God. This book contains his spiritual experiences as a pilgrim repeating the name of Jesus with the formula: *Jesus Christ, Son of God, have mercy on me, a sinner:*

"I walk and say the Jesus Prayer without ceasing and it is more precious and sweet to me than anything else in the world. Sometimes

I walk seventy or more versts a day and I do not get tired; I am only conscious of praying the name of Jesus"[12]

"I was overwhelmed with the desire to recite the Jesus Prayer. And when I started it, it became so easy and delightful that my tongue and lip seemed to do it of themselves. I was joyful the whole day"[13]

"Again I started off on my wanderings. Whenever I happened to meet people during the day, they all seemed as close to me as if they were my kinsmen, even though I did not know them"[14] "Sometimes I experienced a sweet burning in my heart, at other times a burning love for Jesus Christ and all of God's creation. I felt a great joy in calling on the name of Jesus Christ and I realised the meaning of the words: the Kingdom of God is within you (Lk. 17:21)"[15]

"When I began to pray with the heart, everything around me became transformed and I saw it in a new and delightful way. The trees, the grass, the earth, the air, the light, and everything seemed to be saying to me that it exists to witness to God's love for humans and that it prays and sings of God's glory."[16]

English translation: by Helen Bacovcin, *The Way of a Pilgrim*, Image book, Doubleday, New York, 1978.

Malayalam Translation: by Swami Siddhinādhānanada, *Oru Sādhakante Sanchāram*, Ramakrishna Mission, Puranattukara, Trichur, India.

Schimonach Harion was a Russian monk who lived long in Athos, learnt and practiced the Hesychast method of prayer, and after attaining deep spiritual experiences founded a monastery on the banks of the Black Sea. It was called the New Athos. (1875). This gave a new impetus in the spread of Jesus Prayer in the Russian Church. He wrote also a book for common people on the practice of Jesus Prayer. This contributed much to the reception of this form of prayer in wider circles both in Russia and in the Western Church as well.

In the last 60 years Jesus Prayer has been widely received in different parts of the universal Church. In the last 40 years more and more

Christians in Europe are taking to this form of prayer. This is a simple but very effective form that has a deep grounding in the Christian tradition. "The name of Jesus is at the heart of Christian prayer".[17] In the liturgical calendar there is a day devoted to the name of Jesus which goes back to the 6th cent. among the Greeks. In the 7th cent. it spread to France and Italy, and later it was accepted in the universal Church. Now it is celebrated in January.

Pope John Paul II describes Jesus Prayer as the "breath of the soul": "Though it is basically a form of personal prayer, it has a communitarian dimension. It binds the hearts of all, who practice this prayer in a divine bond before the Lord"[18]

Endnotes

[1] S.Painadath SJ, (2014), pp. 153-58.

[2] (for this historical survey we are indebted to the book: Peter Köster, *Die Übung des Herzensgebetes nach der Tradition der Ostkirchen*, EOS Verlag, St. Ottilien, 2007, pp. 49-58).

[3] cit. Gillet (1987), pp. 30-31.

[4] Ruhbach (1989), p. 65.

[5] Pieris SJ (1989), pp. 23-26.

[6] cit. Gillet (1987), p. 36.

[7] Gillet (1987), p. 40.

[8] Canilang (2010), p. 136, 141.

[9] Canilang (2010), p. 184.

[10] cit. Gillet (1987), p. 68.

[11] cit. Gillet (1987), p. 77.

[12] *Way of a Pilgrim* (1978), p. 24.

[13] *Way of a Pilgrim* (1978), p. 22.

[14] *Way of a Pilgrim* (1978), p. 23.

[15] *Way of a Pilgrim* (1978), pp. 40-41.

[16] *Way of a Pilgrim* (1978), p. 34.

[17] Catechism of the Catholic Church (1994). 435.

[18] cit. *L´Osservatore Romano, Nr. 45*, Nov. 06, 1996, p.8.

3

The Inner Mystical Journey

We have seen the historical evolution of Jesus Prayer across the centuries. The great sages were spiritual masters who initiated the aspirants to the path of contemplation and guided them with the prayer of the divine Name. They understood spiritual life as an inner journey taking one to deeper and deeper levels of consciousness. It is a movement from the periphery of the mind to the centre of the soul, from the surface to the depth. At the beginning the invocation of the divine name sounds like a vocal prayer. But in the course of time consciousness gets deepened to an inner silence, the silence of the heart, in which one comes to oneness with the indwelling Christ.

On this inward spiritual journey Asian sages as well as Christian mystics describe the various levels of consciousness. One starts with the upper level of consciousness and slowly moves to the deeper spheres. The inner journey evolves through three spheres: the mind, the psyche and the intuitive faculty.

The Mental Sphere (the conscious level, *manah*)

This is the surface level of awareness; from morning till night one is at this level: *I* am constantly encountering a *thou* or an *it*, persons or things. What steers this extrovert movement is the mind (*manah*) through the five senses. Within the mind there is a twofold activity: to know and to will. Hence the mind is full of thoughts and feelings. Mind can understand something only in as much as the latter is objectified. Mind operates in a subject-object structure. Even if I am trying to understand myself, I have to objectify myself: I have to take myself in the hand. Mind objectifies everything including God.

In this extrovert process of the mind a sense of *I* evolves. This is something constitutive of the human mind. Everyone needs a healthy sense of *I* to accept oneself and to affirm oneself in relation to persons and things. However when the sense of *I* gets fixated on the narrow circle of *I*-and-*mine* feeling, egoism (*aham-kāra*) breeds. It is greed (*kāma*) which fixes the mind on the ego-sense, the desire to possess more and more, not being satisfied with what one has. Buddha said: it is greed (*thrishna*) that causes all suffering in the world. Mahatma Gandhi observed: there is enough for the need of every person on this earth; but there is not enough to satisfy the greed of one person. Emotions, feelings and thoughts evolve in the mind. The decision-making process too takes place in the mind. It is in the mind that one loves and experiences being loved. Human relationships blossom forth in the mind. Joy and sorrow are experienced at the mind level. All socio-cultural and religious activities take place at this mental level of awareness.

The Psychic State (the subconscious level, *Chittha*).

Our inner spiritual journey takes us from the mind down through the psyche. This is the second sphere of consciousness. This psychic state is called the warehouse of the mind, the inner recess of the mind. Memories of the past – personal as well as collective – are stored in this inner ware-house. Several unexpressed emotions and unarticulated thoughts are preserved within this inner recess. There are undigested memories, unfulfilled desires, inner tensions and worries, devastating fears and anxieties, feelings of woundedness, anger and envy in this chamber. These negative emotional forces are like road-blocks on our inner spiritual journey. There are also positive factors like compassion, confidence, gratitude, trust and faithfulness emerging from the psyche and they give quality to human relationships as well. The actions and reactions at the mental level are controlled by the inner-psychic forces (*chittha-vritthih*). These evolve out of the hidden realms of the subconscious. This inner womb of the psyche is shaped by one's own biography, and also through the evolutionary process of humanity (collective unconscious).

21

It is from the psychic level that dreams arise. During the day we live at the level of the mind; while asleep we are in the realm of the psyche. At the mind level there is a strong ego-sense, at the level of the psyche there is no ego-sense: when asleep we do not have the feeling, *I sleep*. If someone says, *I am sleeping*, one is not sleeping! There is no sense of the ego at the second level of consciousness. We cannot fully understand the psychic factors and so we are unable to understand ourselves and control our reactions. This is due to the hidden factors in the psyche.

The Intuitive Consciousness (*nous / buddhi*)

Entry to the third level of consciousness is through the intuitive faculty in us. This is called *nous* in the Greek tradition, *buddhi* in the Indian tradition. This is the inner light of the soul (*antarjyōti, ātmajyōti*). In all religions lamp or flame is the symbol used for buddhi. Jesus said: "The light in you shall not be darkness" (Lk. 11:35). The inner light of the buddhi got illumined in Gautama Siddhartha, and so he became the *buddha*, the enlightened one.

Buddhi is the inner faculty that gives intuition, in-sight, perception of the depth of realities, wisdom. This intuitive faculty brings about enlightenment. Mind is extrovert while buddhi is introspective: turned to the core of reality. Buddhi is the faculty of introspection, intuitive perception. Buddhi leads us to the depth of our existence and renders mystical consciousness.

Buddhi as the intuitive organ is at work in each person. May be, mystics, poets and artists are blessed with a greater share in this inner perception.

Buddhi is often described as:

> 'the inner eye': (*antar-chakshuh, prajnā-nētram, aka-kannu, ullkannu* (Bhagavad Gita).

> "eye of faith" (*oculus fidei*, Augustine)

> 'the third eye' (Saivites / Richard of St. Victor)

'the eye of the heart' (Makarius) [1]

'the inner light' (Upanishads, Bhagavad Gita, John of the Cross)

'the Lotus of the heart' (Upanishads, Buddhism)

Buddhi enables entry into the inner cave of the heart. Buddhi is the door to mystical consciousness. Mystics and sages of all places and times, of all religions and cultures speak of this inner spiritual organ.

The Upanishadic sages make a consistent distinction between the extrovert mind (*manah*) and the introspective faculty of intuition (*buddhi*). The Katha Upanishad gives an impressive image for this: "Body is the chariot and the atman is the Lord of the chariot; the buddhi is the charioteer and the mind is the reins; the senses are the horses" (Kath. Up. 1.3.3-4). Buddhi is attentive to the atman in controlling the senses with the reins of the mind. Buddhi as the spiritual faculty under the inspiration of the divine Atman discerns the movements of the mind and the senses.

On the background of Greek mystical traditions the Church Fathers name the intuitive faculty *nous*.[2]

For Anaxagoras nous is both cosmic intelligence and the human faculty that perceives the harmony of reality (*Phaedo, 97-99*).

Plato describes nous as the spiritual faculty that enables "the vision (*noesis*) of the world of Ideas" (De Legibus, *10, 897b,1*).

According to Aristotle it is through the nous that one intuits (*nus*) the essence of reality (*VEB Phil. Wörterbuch, I*).

In the mystical scheme of Plotinus nous serves as the "transcendent intellect that perceives the ONE in the many" (*The Enneads, 1991, 103*).

According to the Church Fathers it is through the *nous* enlightened by the divine Light, that one perceives the divine dimension of life and reality:

Origen (185-254) said: "The nous, purified and elevated above the material range, sees the Divine and is being divinised by the Divine" (*PG.14, 817a*).

Athanasius (300-373) describes the nous as the medium through which "the human is conjoined (*synaphe*) to the Divine"(*PG. 26. 296b*).

Irenaeus (115-202) speaks of the nous as being "enlightened in order to enjoy the participation in the divine glory" (*Adv, Heres. 4.14.1*).

Gregory of Nyssa (333-394) describes the nous as the mystical organ with which one perceives the divinisation process (*PG. 45, 21d*).

For Augustine (345-430) nous is the "eye of faith" (*oculus fidei*) with which one recognises the working of grace in the soul (*PL. 35.1929*).

Isaac the Syrian calls it "the organ of simple cognition" [3]

The medieval mystics too speak of the inner eye of spiritual perception:

Meister Eckhart (1260-1328) calls it "the spark of the soul" (*Seelenfünklein*), with which one recognises "the birth of God within the inner person." He calls it also the divine eye within: "The eye with which God sees me and the eye with which I see God are but one and the same eye" (*Ave gratia plena*).

Bonaventure (1221-1274) describes it as the "fire within the heart" (*Itinerarium*).

In the classical mystical text *The Cloud of Unknowing* it is "the spiritual eye" that enables the vision through the interior darkness.

Ignatius of Loyola (1491-1556) speaks of the "interior knowledge of the movements of the Spirit" (*Spiritual Exercises 104*).

Theresa of Avila (1515-1582) describes the intuitive faculty as "the door to the interior castle" (*Interior Castle*);

John of the Cross (1542-1591) calls it the "mystical eye" (*Ascent on Mount Carmel*).

The Heart

When the inner light shines forth, when the inner eye of the nous/ buddhi is opened, one looks into the inner recess of reality. This is an ineffable and indescribable experience. This is entry to the sacred space within. Mystics and sages struggle with words and images to describe this divine space. They try to use poetic symbols like:

Cave of the heart (Mundaka Up. 2.2.1)

Space of the heart (Brih. Up. 4.4.22)

City of the Divine (Chand. Up. 8.1.1)

Realm of śūnyata (Buddhism)

Inner garden of the soul (Islamic Sufis)

Interior castle (Theresa of Avila)

Inner space of the soul (Meister Eckhart)

Jesus speaks of it as the 'inner room' in which one truly experiences the Father. "When you pray, go into your inner room, close the door and pray to your Father who is there in silence" (Mt. 6:6). It is in this inner space of the heart that Jesus experienced the Father. Here we experience the true self of our being: the soul, the *jeevātma*. In the Chandogya Upanishad it is said: "In the castle of Brahman, our own body, there is a small shrine in the form of a lotus flower. Within it can be found a small space. We should find the One who dwells there and we should want to know him" (Chand. Up. 8.). This is the spiritual heart, the divine core of the person.

At the mental level we have an ego-sense, (*aham-kāra*); in the heart we have the true self-consciousness, (*ātmabōdha*). Throughout the day we live asserting the *I*. But the sense of the *I* should be rooted in the consciousness of the true self. It is in this consciousness that we realise who we are, and how we are guided by the divine Self from within. From this experience one is drawn to an ever deeper level of consciousness, to the realisation of the Divine in us: the Holy Spirit.

The divine Spirit resides within the heart of all beings, the Divine permeates all beings. The human soul is within the divine Spirit. Ultimately they are ONE. This is the core experience of mystics and sages: the deepest meeting point of the spiritual experiences of all religions.

The spiritual masters of Christianity and of the Asian religions emphasise that the contemplative introspection is ultimately a gift from the Divine. The Divine can be intuited only in the divine light. "In his light we see light" (Ps. 36:9). "You can see the Divine only with the divine eye" (Bhagavad Gita, 11:8). This is a gift of grace. All our spiritual pursuits are a process of opening ourselves to the divine Self, surrendering the soul to the Holy Spirit, tuning the human self (*ātma*) with the divine SELF (*Ātman*).

In this contemplative journey one becomes aware of the Divine as the ultimate subject of the life process. In this mystical consciousness one wakes to the realisation that God is the true subject of our being. This consciousness unfolds within the heart, the core of the human person, the sacred space within us.

Eastern spiritual masters on the heart

Gregory Palamas (1296-1360) describes the heart as "the home of the nous, "the seat of spiritual knowledge", "the innermost body within the body", "the depth of the soul", "the shrine of intelligence", "the throne of grace", "the chief intellectual space of the body", "the abode of the Holy Spirit", "the centre from which the Holy Spirit calls out Abba, Father."[4]

Maximos the Confessor (580-662): "God dwells in the heart of the faithful, and with a pure heart one can see him. (Mt.5:8). God is hidden in the hearts of those who believe in him. The pure heart thus becomes a locus of revelation. If all the power of the Spirit is concentrated in it, the believer is dazzled by a great spiritual splendor and contemplates the Lord in his/her own heart."[5]

Isaac the Syrian (7th cent.): "Enter eagerly into the treasure-house that lies within you and so you will see treasure-house of heaven"[6]

Makarios (330-390): "The heart rules over the whole human organism, and when grace takes possession of the pastures of the heart, it reigns over all a man's thoughts and members. The intellect and all the thoughts of the soul are located there."[7] "The heart is a small vessel, but all things are contained in it: God and the angels, life and the Kingdom of God, the heavenly cities and the treasures of grace."[8]

St. Ephraim (306-373): "Enter within yourself and remain in your heart, for there is God."[9]

Gregory of Sinai (14.cent) calls the heart as the true sanctuary of the divine Spirit.[10]

Theophan the Recluse (1815-1894): "The heart is to be understood in the sense of the *inner man* (Paul). Here dwells the spirit breathed in by God." [11] "To unite the attention and mind with your heart and to remain there unceasingly before the Lord – this is the essential thing in prayer. It is the treasure hidden in the field, the pearl beyond price."[12]

"Only the divine Master of all has the power to enter the heart. When we are in the heart, we are at home. When we are not in the heart, we are homeless."[13] "Every time thoughts begin to confuse you, you have only to descend into the heart and the thoughts will flee."[14] "All your inner disorder is due to the dislocation of the mind and the heart, each going its own way"[15]

"The heart is the innermost man, or spirit. Here are located self-awareness, the conscience, the idea of God and of one's complete dependence on him and all the eternal treasures of the spiritual life."[16]

Modern Authors on the heart

George Maloney SJ: "Deep within you lies a sacred space, your centre, your heart. It is your deepest consciousness, your inner fountain, out of which your highest nature as a spiritual person flows" (*Centering on the Lord Jesus*).

Thomas Merton: "There exists some point at which I can meet God in a real and experiential contact with his infinite actuality. This is the place of God, his sanctuary, the heart. It is a point where my contingent being depends on his love" (*New Seeds of Contemplation*, 37).

Sherrard Palmer in the Glossary of the Philokalia: "The heart in the Philokalia is not simply the physical organ, but the spiritual centre of man´s being: man as made in the image of God, his deepest and true self, the inner shrine, to be entered only through sacrifice and death, in which the mystery of the union between the Divine and the human is consummated."[17]

Endnotes

[1] cit. *Philokalia* (2009), V. 1119.

[2] Painadath SJ (2014), pp. 20-35.

[3] cit. *Philokalia* (2009), V. 111.9

[4] cit. Canilang (2010), p. 188.

[5] cit. Canilang (2010), p. 190.

[6] cit. Chariton (1996), p. 164

[7] cit. Canilang (2010), p. 188.

[8] cit. Chariton (1996), p. 46.

[9] cit. Chariton (1996), p. 182.

[10] *Writings from the Philokalia* (1995) p. 38.

[11] Chariton (1996), p. 191.

[12] cit. *Philokalia* (1996), p. 198.

[13] cit. Chariton (1996), p. 192

[14] cit. Chariton (1996), p.184.

[15] cit. Chariton (1996), p. 195.

[16] cit. Chariton (1996), p. 190.

[17] Philokalia (2009), V, p. 1117.

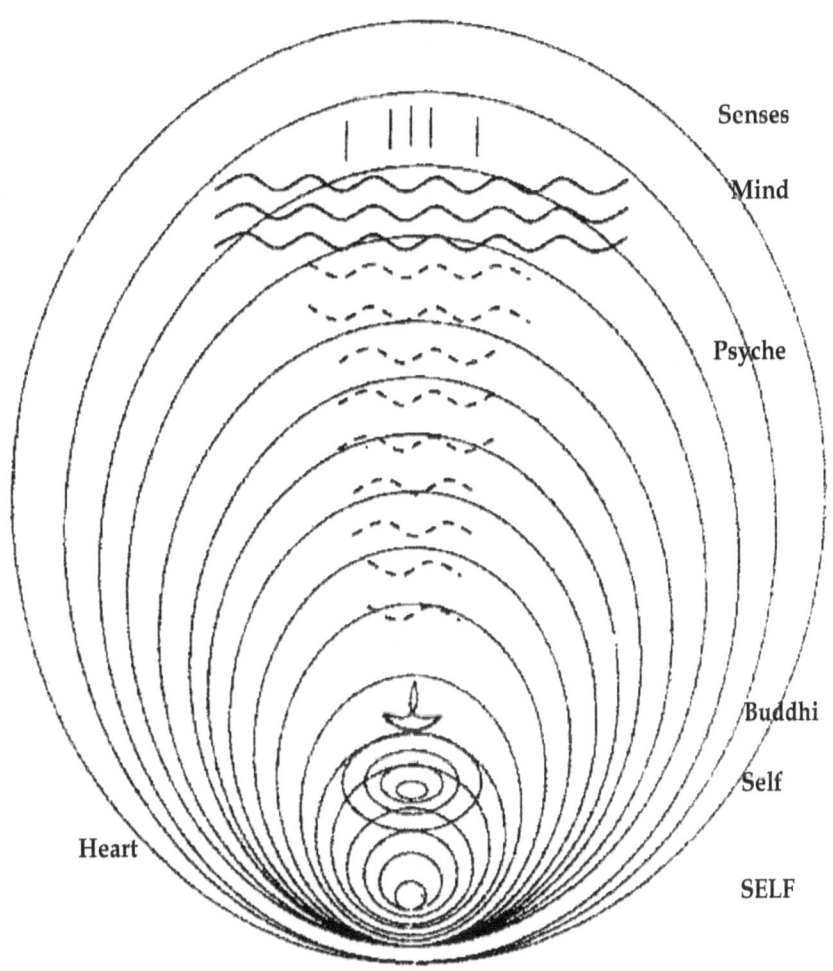

4
Prayer – Meditation – Contemplation

There are three stages on our inner spiritual journey: mental, psychic and intuitive, related to mind (*manah*), psyche (*chittah*) and insight (*buddhi*). Let us examine how prayer evolves through these stages. The inner spiritual journey from the mind to the depth of the soul is like digging a well to reach the hidden springs, like someone diving in the turbulent sea in search of pearls, like a branch waking to the life-giving root, like digging the field to get to the hidden treasure. At the beginning of meditation one needs a lot of personal discipline and effort; but as the process goes on, one becomes increasingly receptive to the divine grace.

The Mental Level: Vocal Prayer

The mind is an extrovert faculty, related to the five senses which bind us to the external world. Knowing, willing, feeling, deciding, imagining, planning, worrying, relishing…all these are activities of the mind. These are expressed through words. When we pray with thoughts and words, the mind is very active. This is mental prayer for we pray at the level of the mind. As we live with the mind and through the mind, we need to pray at the mental level.

Mind objectifies everything: it can grasp something only in as far as it is made into an object. Hence God is also made into an object of worship, a person before us or above us. This cannot be avoided. This is needed for experiencing the divine presence and love. We all look for a tangible experience of God: to feel the loving presence of God, to sense the power of God. For this we need images and symbols, words and codes related to God; these fill our prayer process. All religions communicate this experience of an inter-personal relationship with the Divine: everyone prays!

When we experience God as a *loving God*, our heart blossoms. When we intensely feel that someone loves us, our life becomes beautiful. When we feel that God loves us through Christ in the Spirit, our life gets a new quality. This is communicated through personalised images of God and Christ. God becomes a divine *thou* for the human *I*. We see God as a person before us or above us. This calls for a response of surrender, *bhakti*, love, obedience. This response is articulated in words: we pray to this God. Hence we invoke God as Father, Lord, Master and Redeemer in prayer. We pray to God the Father, to Christ the Lord. An intense inter-personal relationship grows between the human person and God. In prayer we meet God as *thou* before us and above us.

There is a marked difference between mental prayer and meditation. What we often call meditation with biblical texts is not actually meditation; it is rather discursive prayer: reflection on the biblical words. It is mental prayer because the mind is activated with thinking, imagining and deciding. Here words, thoughts and prayers are important. This is needed at the initial stage to understand the biblical text in depth. This is not *dhyāna* but *manana*, the first stage in the spiritual journey.

The Psychic Level: Prayer of the Name

Our inner spiritual journey does not end at the upper level of the mind. The journey takes us to the deeper levels: to the sub-conscious and unconscious realms. This journey goes through the inner jungle of the psyche. Here we meet with undigested memories, unfulfilled desires, inner tensions and worries, devastating fears and anxieties, feelings of woundedness, anger and envy...all sorts of negative emotional forces may come up. They are like road-blocks on our inner spiritual journey through the jungle of the psyche.

No one likes to go through the jungle all alone. One would look for a guide: someone who has gone ahead, who knows the way, someone who has the strength to take us through the forest. This is where Indian masters and Christian mystics recommend the practice of the prayer of the divine Name. By repeating the name of the divine Master we surrender ourselves unconditionally to the guidance and power of the Lord. Jesus Prayer is a powerful form of prayer to go through the jungle of the psyche.

Prayer may begin with a lot of words, intentions, praise and thanksgiving. Gradually the words get reduced to perhaps just one word, one phrase. Further, as the inner journey enters the inner psyche, even that word is left behind. One takes up the name of the Lord in a form that resonates with the inner realm. It is important that the name is repeated, with deep love, adoration and surrender, and with an inner melody as well, so that vibrations are evoked.

When we devoutly repeat the name of Jesus we surrender ourselves to Christ, the divine Master in us. He is the one who guides us to the depth of mystical consciousness. When in the course of this inner journey disturbing memories or distracting thoughts arise, we surrender them to the divine Master. We remain relaxed as he is guiding us. The negative feelings from the sub-conscious surface and these are being purified by the vibrations of the divine Name. Utter trust in the divine guide is the real solution to the problem of inner disturbances and utter loneliness. The real psychic healing comes from within the divine well-springs.

The Intuitive Level: Meditation

As the mind comes to rest and the psyche attains certain serenity, consciousness sinks to the level of the buddhi: the inner faculty of intuition, in-sight. It is through the buddhi that deep God-consciousness evolves. "Buddhi is the point at which the human mind is open to the divine light. If buddhi turns towards the light it is illumined by the divine light and transmits the light to the mind and the senses. But if the buddhi is turned away from the light then the mind is darkened and the personality is divided. Buddhi is also the point of unification of the personality. It is here that we become fully human."[1]

The English word meditation comes from the Latin verb *meditari*, which means to go to the centre. The Sanskrit word for meditation is *dhyāna*, which literally means journey (*yāna*) to the intuitive perception (*dhi*=buddhi). *Dhi* + *yāna* means journey through / to the intuitive faculty. The meditative journey is a spiritual pilgrimage through the buddhi to the divine centre of one's being.

In order to get the consciousness open to buddhi, Indian masters recommend the use of mantras. Mantra is not a word, nor a name. Mantra has no conceptual meaning that the mind grasps. Mantra is a means by which the mind can be transcended. (*mananāt trāyatē iti mantra* = that which goes beyond the mind is mantra). Mantra does not evoke meaning, but it creates vibrations. Being spiritually potential mantra brings about divine vibrations in the inner realms.

Of all the mantras the primordial mantra is OM. It consists of three primal sounds: A, U and M. A= beginning / the very first sound that one can produce, U= middle, and M= end / the closing humming sound. (A + U = O). OM signifies therefore the totality, the all comprehending power, the all-pervading divine presence. OM is the sound symbol of the divine omnipresence. OM is the articulation of the divine vibration in the cosmos, the expression of the divine creativity, the syllable of the divine presence here and now. By repeating OM one enters into a deep silence within the *cave of the heart*, the divine space within us. The Upanishadic masters use the imagery of bow and arrow: the repetition of OM is the bow, the soul is the arrow, that straightaway penetrates the divine goal (Mundaka Up. 2.2.4).

When the name of Jesus is repeated with the mantra OM, powerful spiritual vibrations evolve within us. The transforming effect of the divine Name is intensified through the mantra OM. The power of the Holy Spirit immanent in the name *Jesus* flows out when the name is chanted meditatively with the divine sound *OM*. Slowly consciousness sinks into the heart.

The Heart Level: Contemplation

One thus enters the inner divine space through the door of the buddhi; this is entry into the heart. On prayer process Jesus said: "go into your inner room, close the door and commune with the Divine in silence" (Mat. 6:6). It is in the sacred realm of the heart, that we experience the presence of the Divine as inner light, as inner fountain, ground of being, root of being, as Father-Mother, as supreme Self (*Paramātma*), as the divine Spirit. True prayer, Jesus said, evolves "in Spirit and truth" (Jn. 4:24). The word truth in Greek (*aletheia*) means openness. Our God experience then evolves in total openness to the Spirit, in letting the Spirit pray in deep silence (Rom. 8:27). This is contemplation. In contemplation we have a trans-personal relationship with the Divine. We go beyond name and form. Only the vibrant divine presence is felt. We experience the Divine as the true subject of our being. This is the way Jesus experienced the Father: I draw life from the Father, the words which I speak are not mine, but of the Father, who dwells within me (Jn. 6:57, 14:10). In this contemplative experience God is not someone who is in front or above me, but he is the indwelling presence. Mystics and sages of all religions make consistently a distinction between *God* and the *Divine*. Initially one meets God as personal thou before oneself, but gradually one realises that the Divine is the ultimate reality within oneself. *God* as object becomes the *Divine* as subject; *God* as person becomes the *Divine* as presence within. This is the transition from prayer through meditation to contemplation, from active vocal prayer to receptive silence in contemplation, from words to deep intuitive silence, from mind to the heart.

Be present to the present moment of the Divine - it is in this state that we receive deep insights, which give us inner light, strength and conviction. These deepen our consciousness. These are powerful moments. This is *jnāna*. *Jnāna* (wisdom) makes us capable of transforming our life. It enlightens us to make important decisions and stand by them. There is a difference between *vi-jnāna* and *jnāna*. *Vi-jnāna* is discursive knowledge that one attains with external helps at the mind level; *jnāna* is wisdom that one receives as grace at the buddhi level; *vijnāna* is information from outside, *jnāna* is experience from within.

An integrated spiritual process demands both the inter-personal encounter with the divine Lord in the mind and a trans-personal experience of the divine Spirit in the heart. Out of the inter-personal encounter evolves the response of devotional self-surrender, *bhakti*; out of the experience of oneness comes mystical union, contemplative introspection, *jnāna*. Through the integration of bhakti and *jnāna* evolves karma: one gets engaged for the welfare of the world in works of justice and compassion.

Inter-personal and Trans-personal Dimensions of Prayer

Inter-personal Relationship at the mental level	Trans-personal Experience within the heart
Inter-personal relationship evolves at the mind level	Tans-personal experience unfolds in the buddhi /nous
Mind evokes concrete forms of God	Buddhi is open to the incomprehensible / ineffable divine mystery
God is experienced as a personal thou	The Divine is experienced as presence
Prayer to the personal God	Contemplation of the divine presence
The dominant role of activity, words, thoughts, imagination, images...	Characterised by silence, receptivity, attentiveness to the groaning of the Spirit
Invoking God with names and forms: Father, Master, Saviour, Lord...	Experiencing the Divine as pure presence beyond all names and forms
Vocal prayer, rituals, praise, worship, adoration	Contemplative silence, attentiveness to the pure presence of the Divine
Loving surrender to the divine Lord in devotion (*bhakti*)	Awareness of the divine presence in gnosis (*jnāna*)
Devotional religiosity in relation to the divine Lord	Mystical spirituality in the awareness of the Divine presence
Duality dominates: God before me	Union with the Divine within me
Searching for the will of God in response to the commandments of God	Resonating with the divine vibrations and inspirations
Static images of God dominate	Dynamic and transforming process is vital

Horizontal orientation in subject-object relationship	Vertical immersion to the Divine as ultimate subject
Like relatedness among the branches: horizontal relationship with others	Like rootedness in the Ground of being: relationship from vertical union
We are different like branches	We are one within the divine Ground
Knowledge about God (*vijnāna*)	Wisdom of the Divine (*jnāna*)
One struggles with a lot of distractions and psychic turbulence	One experiences inner peace, serenity, joy and bliss
Dependence on a particular form of God at the mind level	Inner freedom and strength to move with the inspiration of the Spirit
Question: "Where do I worship God, in Jerusalem or on this mountain?"	Response: "Worship God in Spirit and Truth"
Doing: active	Being: receptive
Swinging with the fluctuations of the mind between the past and future	Always in the present: no time consciousness, "eternal now"
Human effort dominates	Divine Grace overwhelms
The danger of manipulation in devotional practices: politicisation, commercialisation, demonstrativeness in religious practices	The danger of withdrawal and self-sufficiency, hyper-critical of religious forms and structures, elitist mindset

Endnotes

1 Griffiths (1982), p. 71.

II

5

The Divine Consciousness of Jesus

We have been exploring the inner spiritual journey from the mind to the heart. We noticed three phases:

Prayer in the I-thou structure at the mental level (through words / praise / adoration/ rituals / vocal prayer....)

Meditation as the transition from the mind to the nous / buddhi (prayer of the divine Name, the repetition of mantra, the interiorisation of symbols ...)

Contemplation deep inner silence in which we experience the oneness with the Divine in the heart.

Now we pursue the inner journey of Jesus because Jesus Christ is for us Christians „the Way, the Truth and the Life" (Jn.14: 6). Seekers of other religions have their spiritual pursuits with enlightening names and salvific symbols, which we sincerely respect. How did Jesus go into the deeper levels of consciousness? What did he experience within the heart? Whom did Jesus call the *Father*? What is the spiritual experience that Jesus wanted to communicate to us?

The Inner Journey of Jesus

It is in the Gospel of John that we have a certain access to the inner mystical experience of Jesus. Being a mystic himself, John sensed the depth of the mystical experience of Jesus. And being the beloved disciple, John had the privilege of being closer to the interior life and struggles of the divine Master. (Jn. 13:23, 19:26). In the deep moments of ecstasy (Transfiguration on the Mount) and in the intense moments of agony (Gethsemane, Calvary) John stood close to Jesus. While retiring to places of solitude Jesus must have often taken John with him. (Jn. 1:39, Lk.9:28). John could then watch closely how the

Master sank into deep contemplative silence and communed with the divine source of his life. Jesus must have shared with John some of his deepest spiritual experiences. (Jn. 21:22, 25). This seems to explain why John could describe the inner search and struggles of Jesus as well as the intense experience of Jesus' being one with the Father.

The Gospel of John communicates the inner experience of Jesus with beautiful symbols. Let us take up three symbols for a meditative reflection: the tree, the well and the word.

The Tree

Jesus spoke of himself as the vine-stock: "I am the vine, you are the branches" (Jn. 15:5). No vine-stock or trunk of a tree stands by itself; it is supported and enlivened by the roots hidden in the mother earth. From the root the vital sap flows through the trunk to the branches and the tree grows flowers and produces fruits.

The hidden root is the life-giving source of the trunk. Jesus experienced the mysterious Divine as the root of his being, the divine ground and foundation of his being. This he called the *Father*. In the language of the trunk Jesus said:

"I draw life from the Father" (6:57),

"I am sent forth by the Father" (17:8, 8:42),

"The one who sent me is with me" (8:16),

"I am in the Father, and the Father is in me" (14:10),

"I come forth from the Father" (8:42)

"From him I am" (7:29).

Just as the trunk experiences the life-giving root, Jesus experienced the Father as the source of his being. It is the trunk that lets the vital sap flow from the root to the branches; Jesus experienced himself to be the manifestation of the invisible presence of the Divine to humanity. As the trunk is the self-expression of the hidden root within the earth Jesus experienced himself to be the self-revelation, the self-communication, and the manifestation of the incomprehensible, invisible, mysterious presence of the Father to humanity. In this realisation Jesus said:

"Anyone who sees me, sees the Father" (14:9),

"Anyone who knows me, knows the Father" (14:7),

"Anyone who hears me, hears the Father" (14:10),

"Anyone who welcomes me, welcomes the Father" (13:20),

"Anyone who listens to me, listens to the Father" (8:47),

"Anyone who believes in me, believes in the Father" (12:44).

Jesus realised his conscious oneness with the Father. The Father is the subject of the Son, the true self of his being. Jesus spoke with an abiding consciousness of being the voice of the Father. The Father is the true self, the subject that speaks and works through the Son. In this subject-consciousness Jesus could say:

"I perform the works of my Father" (5:36),

"I have come to do the will of him who sent me" (6:38).

In the deepest subject-consciousness he exclaimed: "The Father and I are one" (10:30). There is no existence for the Son separate and apart from the Father. The awareness of this oneness is the source of all the works and words of Jesus. Jesus had the realisation that he is the Son of God. He lived out of this consciousness of being the Son of God. From the root the trunk comes forth through the flow of the vital sap; in this sense the trunk is the daughter / son of the root. Jesus had the consciousness of being the Son of God.

What makes the root give birth to the trunk is the vital sap of the tree. Constantly the life-giving sap flows from the root to the trunk and to the branches. The vital sap is the symbol of the Holy Spirit. Throughout the Bible water is the symbol of the divine Spirit.

"Let anyone who is thirsty come to me and drink; from his heart shall flow streams of living water; Jesus was referring to the Spirit" (Jn. 7:37-38)

"No one can enter the Kingdom of God without being born through water and the Spirit" (Jn. 3:5)

"I shall pour clean water over you and you will be cleansed" (Ez. 36:25)

"My people have abandoned me, the fountain of living water" (Jer. 2:13)

Like the life-giving fluid of the tree the Spirit flows from the Father to the Son and through the Son to the Father (*perichoresis*). The Spirit makes the Father give birth to the Son; the Spirit is the power of life, stream of love within the Divine.

Jesus experienced himself as the out-growth of the divine trunk (Son) into the world, born of the divine root (Father) and nourished by the divine sap (Spirit).

The Well

Well is another symbol which reveals the divine consciousness of Jesus. Much of what is said with the symbol of the tree is applicable to that of the well. When Jesus spoke with the Samaritan woman at Jacob's well, (Jn. 4:13-14) and also at Jerusalem when he preached to the pilgrims at the festival of Tabernacles (7:37-38), the symbol of the well is clearly brought out. Jesus said: "Those who are thirsty come and drink from me" – Here, Jesus describes himself as a well that offers the waters of divine life.

A well is the outpouring of the springs hidden in the mother earth. Just as a well manifests the hidden springs in the earth, Jesus realised himself to be the manifestation of the divine spring within him. Jesus called the divine spring the *Father*. The Father is invisible, incomprehensible and mysterious. "No one has ever seen the Father" (5:37). Through Jesus the Father is revealed. Hence he said:

"I come forth from the Father" (8:14, 42),

"The Father who is the source of life has made the Son the source of life" (5:26).

Jesus experienced within himself the Divine as the hidden spring. In the way the well speaks about the springs, Jesus spoke of the presence of God within himself. In reality the well is the daughter / son of the spring. Jesus had the consciousness of being the Son of God, the Self-revelation of the Divine. What makes the hidden springs unfold in the well is the inherent current, the power of the out-flow. This is the symbol of the divine Spirit. Jesus alludes to this as he said: "Streams of living water will flow through you, this is the Spirit" (7, 37-39). The Spirit is the life-energy (*energia*) in the Divine.

The Word

It is mainly through words that a person communicates with others. Every word is born out of the womb of silence. Thought emerges from the mysterious depth of silence. Jesus experienced the Divine within him as the eternal, mysterious silence. "No one has ever heard his voice" (5:37; 8: 14). Son is the Word (*logos*) that verbalises the divine silence. Jesus spoke with an abiding consciousness of being the voice of the Father.

"My teaching is not from myself; it comes from the one who sent me" (7:16),

"What I say is what the Father has taught me" (8:28),

"What I say to you, I do not speak of my own accord: it is the Father living in me doing his works" (14:10),

"The word that you hear is not my own: it is the word of the Father who sent me" (14:24),

"I have not spoken of my own accord; but the Father who sent me commanded me what to say and what to speak; what the Father has told me is what I speak" (12:49-50).

The Father is the true Self that speaks through the Son. The Father is the eternal silence behind the Word that is born out of it. The Word is the articulation of silence. What fills the silence and the Word is the meaning / the content / the truth. This is the symbol of the Holy Spirit, the Spirit of Truth. The Spirit is the Truth contained in the divine Word. (14:17, 15:26). What the Son communicates from within the Father is the divine Truth, the Spirit. The literal meaning of the word Truth (*aletheia*) is opening, uncovering, unfolding. The Spirit unfolds the mystery of the Divine. The Spirit is the immanent power that makes the Father generate the Son. "The Spirit explores the depths of everything, even the depths of God" (I. Cor. 2:10). Jesus experienced himself as the expression of the divine Word (Son), that articulates the divine silence (Father) and communicates the divine Truth (Spirit).

The Poetic Symbols of the Early Church Fathers

The early Church Fathers used such poetic symbols to speak of Jesus' consciousness and on the Trinity.

Tertullian said:

> "God brought forth the Word as the root brings forth the shoot, as the spring brings forth the stream, as the sun brings forth the beam of light. Each of these manifestations is an outflow of being from its respective source: the shoot is the son of the root, the stream is the son of the spring, the beam of light is the son of the sun." (*Adv. Praxeam, 8*).

Origen: "The Son is derived from the fountainhead of the Father" (*On John 2.2.10*).

Athanasius: "The Son is like the radiance from the sun, like the stream from the fountain, like the word from silence" (*PG. 26,328*).

Hyppolitus: "The Son comes out of the Father as water from a fountain, as ray from the sun" (*PG. 10,817*).

Ambrose: "The Son is begotten from the womb of the Father *(de utero Patris)*. The Father is the fountain and root of the Son´s being" *(PL. 16,642)*.

Tertullian: "The Spirit proceeds like fruit, proceeding from the root through the bud" *(Adv. Praxeam, 4)*.

Athenagoras: "The Son is the wisdom of the Father, and the Spirit is the effulgence as light from fire" *(PG. 6,945)*.

Ignatius of Antioch: "Out of the eternal silence God spoke his Word" *(Letter to Ephesians, 19, 1)*.

These three symbols reveal the divine consciousness of Jesus that he is the manifestation or expression of the hidden and mysterious presence of the Father. Just as the trunk unfolds the hidden root, just as the well opens up the hidden springs, just as the word articulates the silence, the Son is the self-communication of the Father: the outgrowth of the divine root, the outpouring of the divine fountain, the articulation of the divine eternal silence. The Son is "the image of the unseen God" (Col. 1:15).

The Dimensions of Experience

In the God-consciousness of Jesus three dimensions can be noticed:

(i) "The Father sent me", "I come forth from the Father (Jn. 3:17, 4:34, 5:36-38, 7:28-29, 10:36, 17:3). Jesus had an abiding consciousness of being sent by the Father. Here the Father is the one who sends the Son with the redemptive mission. The Son understands his mission as 'doing the will of the Father' (4:34, 5:30, 6:38), as 'completing the work of the Father' (6:29; 5:19, 10:37, 17:4). What is perceived here is a certain distinction between the one who sends and the one who is sent. The relation between the Father and the Son is an *inter-personal* relation.

(ii) "I am in the Father and the Father is in me" (5:26, 8:28, 14:10; 17:21, 23). Jesus knew that the Father who sent him is with him, in him (8:16, 29, 16:32, 14:10). Here the Father is the one who gives life to the Son from within. The Son constantly takes birth from the Father (5:26; 6:57; 8:42; 16:28). The Father is the source of life for the Son, the ground of his being. Between them there is total mutual immanence, intense com-penetration (*perichoresis*). The Son is the expression and unfolding of the Father (14:10; 12:49). There is no Father without the Son, no Son without the Father. The relation between the Father and the Son is an *intra*-personal relation.

(iii) "The Father and I are One" (10:30; 17:11, 21, 22). This is the articulation of the deepest experience of Jesus in relation to the Divine. Jesus had the consciousness that his being and life and work have been totally transparent to the divine source, the Father. Father and Son are essentially one. The Son is the self-communication / manifestation of the Father. The relation between the Father and the Son is a *trans*-personal relation, in the sense that it goes far beyond the personality structures of the human mind.

These three aspects of Jesus' consciousness may not be taken as three phases or spheres, but as the three integral dimensions of his God consciousness.

Indian Perception

The vedantic sages speak of three dimensions of God-consciousness:

(i) I and the Divine are two. The human and the Divine are experienced as two realities. This is the experience of duality (*dvaita*). Bhakti, worship, rituals, offerings, love, surrender are all expressions of this.

(ii) I am a particle of the Divine. Here the emphasis is on participation, on the indwelling presence. The human is the abode of the Divine, part of the Divine. This is the experience of qualified-nonduality (*viśishtādvaita*).

(iii) I am one with the Divine. Here the emphasis is on unity, on ONE-ness. The human is totally one with the Divine. In fact there is no reality second to the Divine. The Divine is the one and only existence, there is no second one (*advaita*).

All the three are integral dimensions of any genuine God experience: one cannot be isolated from the other. These may also be phases in everyone's search for the Divine. In the inner journey of Jesus all the three dimensions can be found: he experienced his mission as being *sent* by the Father, his life *within* the Father and his being *one* with the Father.

The Transforming Process in Jesus

How did Jesus arrive at this divine consciousness? How did Jesus in his inner journey enter into the divine core of his life? It has been often narrated by the evangelists, that Jesus used to retire to the solitude of the mountain, to the silence of the night, to commune with the Father. In the stillness of the night he spent many hours in communion with his Father in silent meditation: the sea-shore, the river-banks, the fields, the woods were all places of intense communion with his Father (Lk.5:16; 6:12; 11:1; 6:1-17; 13:10; 14:17. Mt. 5:1; 8:20; 26:55. Mk. 2:2; 4:1; 11:17).

Jesus lived constantly in contemplative intimacy with the divine ground, the Father. He experienced himself as the transparent medium transmitting divine life to the world. Hence he could say on the first step to his public ministry: "The Spirit of the Lord is upon me, for he has sent me forth to bring Good News to the poor..." (Lk. 4:18). It was the will of the Father that was accomplished through him. Jesus' total self-surrender to the Father meant total death to the ego in him: "The grain of wheat has to fall on the ground and die, so that new life sprouts forth from it" (Jn. 12:24). His entire life was a continuous process of death and resurrection. Cross and resurrection were not just events at the end of his life, but they meant an ongoing process of the human in him increasingly becoming transparent to the Divine in him. This has been a transforming process which involved much suffering. From the human side this meant surrender of the human ego to the divine Self. "During his life on earth, he offered up prayer and entreaty, with loud cries and with tears, to Him who had the power to save him from death, and he was heard because of his godly fear. Though he was Son, he learnt obedience through suffering" (Heb. 5:7). The agony in Gethsemane (Mt. 26:38-39) and on the Cross (Mt. 27:46) have been moments of intense suffering. And from the divine side this meant self-emptying (*kenosis*). "Though being in the form of God, he did not count equality with God as something to be grasped; but he emptied himself, taking the form of a slave, becoming as human beings are; and being in every way like a human being, he humbled himself, even to accepting death, death on a cross" (Phi. 2:6-8).

Jesus invited his disciples to follow him; this ultimately meant losing one´s life and growing unto the Divine. "Anyone who wants to save his life, will lose it; but anyone who loses his life for my sake, and for the sake of the Gospel, will save it" (Mk. 8:35). This is an invitation to enter into the same transformative process that took place in him, so that the disciples too experience oneness with the Father, just as Jesus experienced it. "May they all be one, just as you are in me and I am in you, so that they also may be in us; may they be so perfected in oneness, so that the world may recognise that you have loved them as you loved me" (Jn. 17:21.23). Jesus Prayer is a simple but powerful way to enter into this experience of oneness.

The Tri-une God

Meditation on these mystical symbols of Jesus' inner experience throws some light on the mystery of the Divine as Trinity.

(i) The Father as Mystery. The root, well-spring and silence point to the aspect of hiddenness. There is no direct access to any of these. The symbol of the *Father* refers to the ineffable mystery of the Divine. Jesus experienced the Father primarily as the divine mystery within him. "The Father is greater than I" (14:28). In fact the root is deeper than the trunk, the hidden springs are more than the outflow, and silence is richer than words. No concrete self-expression of the Divine can give us a full access to the divine mystery. "No one has seen the Father; no one has heard his voice" (5:37). The Father as the *whence* of the Son always remains an incomprehensible mystery for us. At the same time the Father is the symbol of the source of divine life. The Son is born from the *womb* of the Father (Ambrose). God as Father is the generating *mother-base* of the Divine. Jesus lived out of this consciousness of the Father: "I come out of the Father" (8:42; 16:28), "I draw life from the Father" (6:57).

(ii) The Son as the Expression. The second element of the three symbols points to the self-unfolding of the Divine. The trunk unfolds the hidden root, the well opens up the hidden springs, the word articulates the silence. The Son is the self-communication of the Father: the outgrowth of the divine root, the outpouring of the divine fountain, the articulation of the mystery of divine silence. The Son is the 'the image of the unseen God' (Col. 1:15), the language of the Divine. Jesus lived out of this consciousness of being the Son of God.

"Anyone who sees me, sees the Father" (14:9),

"Anyone who knows me, knows the Father" (14:7),

"Anyone who hears me, hears the Father" (14:10).

In Jesus Christ we see with the eyes of faith the Word incarnate, the face of God turned towards humanity, the hand of God stretched out to embrace the estranged world. Jesus is *Immanuel*, God-with-us here and now.

(iii) The Spirit as the Power. What is communicated through these three symbols is in fact the immanent power of life. Through the trunk the vital sap flows from within the womb of the root; through the well / river the refreshing water is poured out from the springs; through the word the truth is articulated from the silence of the mind.

Through the Son the divine Spirit is sent forth from the Father. It is by the power of the Spirit that the Father generates the Son. The Spirit permeates the Father and the Son as the immanent divine energy (*perichoresis*). The Spirit explores the depth of the Divine (I Cor. 2:10).

The Spirit is the self-communication of the divine life (6:63),

the self-manifestation of the divine light (8:12),

the self-revelation of the divine truth (14:17),

the self-outpouring of the divine love (Rom. 5:5).

Jesus experienced himself as the channel of the divine Spirit. He was born of the Spirit (Lk. 1:35), brought up by the Spirit (Lk.1:80), filled with the Spirit (Lk. 4:1), anointed by the Spirit (Lk.4:18), led by the Spirit (Lk. 4:14), enlightened by the Spirit (Lk.10:21) and empowered by the Spirit (Mt. 12:28). Jesus lived out of a deep consciousness of the Father as the subject of his being (Jn. 14:10) and of the Spirit as the power within himself (Mt.12:28). In this sense Jesus Christ is the self-outpouring of the divine Spirit in the world. Hence he could say the inviting words: "Those who are thirsty come and drink from me; out of the centre of your being shall flow streams of the divine Spirit" (Jn.7:37-39).

The Divine as Self-Communication

The inner journey of Jesus offers the light to look into the abysmal mystery of the Divine and realise the Trinitarian process therein. In his light we see light. In his experience we experience the Divine. When we look into the *depths of the Divine* in the light of the experience of Jesus, we realise that the Divine is a self-giving reality. Divine life is a self-unfolding process: like the root unfolding itself through the trunk, like the hidden springs pouring out as the stream, like the silence articulating itself in the word. These mystical symbols point to the truth: the Trinitarian Divine is not a static reality, but a constant self-outpouring of life. God is not like a self-contained lake resting in itself on the mountaintop, but like a lake that continuously pours itself out into the river; the lake however continues to be lake for it is nourished by the hidden springs (John Chrysostom). God as Trinity means that God is Love: love is self-giving. God as Trinity means God is a Living God: life is a self-transcending process. In this process of the inner-Trinitarian life three dimensions may be recognised: to be within itself, to go out of itself, to return to itself. Similarly in the process of love too three dimensions are present: to be within myself, to go out of myself to the thou, and to return to me. In as much as one could discern reflections of the trinity (*vestigia trinitatis*) in the human experience of life and love one may speak of the Trinity as follows:

God-within-self (*entstasis*) – this is the Father
God-out-of-self (*ekstasis*)– this is the Son
God-unto-self (*dynamis*) – this is the Spirit.

> Father is the *I*
> Son is the *Thou*
> Spirit is the *We*.

God above all – this is the Father
God through all – this is the Son
God in all – this is the Spirit (cfr. Eph. 4:6).

> Father is the beginningless beginning
> Son is the self-communication of God
> Spirit is the healing presence of God

Father is the Ground and Abyss of the Divine
Son is the freedom and love of the Divine
Spirit is the communion and relationality of the Divine.

> Father refers to the dimension of transcendence
> Son points to the dimension of immanence
> Spirit conveys the dimension of transparency.

The eternal Silence of the Divine – this is the Father

The eternal Word of the Divine – this is the Son

The eternal Wisdom of the Divine – this is the Spirit.

One does not come after the other; all the three dimensions are always ONE, yet three. Father, Son and Spirit are ONE, yet three: one in being (*homousios, consubstantial*) and yet there is a distinction of the three (*hypostaseis / prosopa /personae*). "Each in each, each in all, all in each, all in all, all in ONE" (Augustine, *De Trinitate, 7.6.11*). "One with one, one from one, one in one and One eternal" (Meister Eckhart, *Vom edlen Menschen*). "We hold the distinction, not the confusion of Father, Son and Holy Spirit: a distinction without separation, a distinction without plurality" (Ambrose, *To Gratian, 4,8*). The Trinitarian mystery reveals that the Divine is not one-alone (*unus*), but ONE (*unum*), not *ēkah* but *ēkam*, not solitary but communion. The divine unity is triune. The use of the neutral in designating the oneness, shows that there is a dynamism within the ONE.

6
Divinisation of the Human

We have examined the process of the introspective spiritual journey and looked at the way Jesus went on this inner journey: Jesus experienced the Divine as the Father, and himself as the self-expression of the Divine, and the Spirit as the power of love. Now let us focus on what Jesus wanted to communicate to us.

The Symbol of the Tree

Let us look at the symbol of the tree. The vital sap that flows from the root to the trunk flows further upward into all the branches. Just as the trunk is conjoined to the root the branches are conjoined to the trunk. Just as the trunk grows out of the root the branches grow out of the trunk. Ultimately there is no difference between the relationship of the trunk with the root and the relationship of the branches with the trunk. The root, the trunk and the branches are of one nature.

Keeping this symbol in mind we could sense the deeper mystical meaning of the sayings of Jesus as found in the Gospel according to John:

> "*Just as* the Father sent me into the world, so do I send you into the world" (17:18),
>
> "*Just as* the Father knows me, I know my own" (10:15),
>
> "*Just as* the Father has loved me, so have I loved you" (15:9; 17:26),
>
> "*Just as* I remain in the love of the Father, so will you remain in my love" (15:10),
>
> "*Just as* I draw life from the Father, so will you draw life from me" (6:57),

"Just as I am in the Father, and the Father is in me, so am I in you and you are in me" (17:21;14:20),

Just as the Father and I are one, so may you all be one in us" (17-21-22).

(*kathos* = *Just as*)

Jesus wanted that all those who believe in him make the same inner journey that he made, and participate in the same inner experience that shaped his consciousness. Jesus wants us to realise that we are daughters / sons of God. It is the realization that the divine presence which unfolded itself in Jesus continues the self-unfolding in us all. It is the awareness that the same divine Spirit that filled and moved Jesus fills and moves all those who wake up to this divine consciousness. It is the enlightened consciousness that we are branches of the divine Tree and streams of the divine well-springs.

The New Life in Christ

All this means liberation from a superficial, ego-centered, consumerist self-identity to a deeper, God-centered, and holistic self-realisation: liberation from 'life according to the flesh' (*sarkikos*) to 'life according to the Spirit' (*pneumatikos*) (Rom. 8:5-8; Gal. 5:18-24). "Anyone who holds on to his life will lose it; anyone who loses his life for my sake will save it for eternal life." (Mk.8:35; Jn. 12:25). "Unless the grain of wheat falls into the ground and die it remains alone; if it dies it sprouts for into new life" (Jn. 12:24-26).

One has to be reborn into a deeper self-consciousness: 'reborn in Spirit and water' (3:1). This is an invitation to a divine consciousness, to the discovery of one's true self-identity within the inner-trinitarian divine life-process. Our life unfolds not so much before God as within the Divine, *just as* the branches unfold from the root through the stem in the flow of the vital sap. This is the meaning of baptism referred to at the end of the Gospel of Mathew. The Latin Vulgate translation *in nomine* does not render the dynamic meaning of the

56

Greek original *eis to onoma,* which would mean: initiate them *into* the life of the Father-Son-Spirit.[1] Baptism is not just a ritual but a way of life. Just as the Father is the source and fountain of Jesus, Jesus becomes the source and fountain of our life.

The divine Spirit transforms our life into the divine life. The divine sap (the Spirit) that flows from the root (the Father) through the trunk (the Son) enlivens all the branches and leaves, i.e. all who are inserted to the trunk. Our life merges with the divine life; our being is rooted on the divine Ground; our existence is enlivened by the hidden divine springs. The ego-sense has to be transcended unto a divine self-consciousness; this divine self-consciousness becomes the source of light and strength, love and joy in our life.

In the light of Jesus´s experience of the Divine we can also open ourselves to the mystical depth of experience: God as the Subject within us, that-out-of-which we live. Such an experience renders our life with a divine axis. Then our activities get a divine horizon, a divine dimension, a divine meaning: they become truly participation in the divine work of renewing this world. We become instruments in the hands of the divine Spirit. God works through us. Then we are able to make decisions with a deeper consciousness, not just to please the demands of the ego, but to respond to the call of the true self within. We can then discern God´s will in our decision making process. The inner light shines through and enlightens our paths. We are contemplatives in action and active out of contemplation.

Jesus the Way

Jesus presented himself as the *way* to this process of realization. He awakens in us the divine consciousness that unfolded in him. Our relationship to Christ has to grow deeper than the mere I-thou relationship. Our life unfolds *in Christ*. This becomes clear when we meditate on the Christ-symbols associated with the *I am* statements of Jesus. These are not just objectifying symbols, but assimilative symbols:

"I am the bread of life" (Jn. 6:35, 48). Bread is not an object to be kept on the table, but something to be eaten and assimilated.

"I am the living water" (4:14). Water is not just to be preserved in a bottle, but to drink and quench the thirst.

"I am the light" (8:12). We do not see light as an object, rather we see everything in the light.

"I am the way, the door" (14:6, 10:7). The way is for us to go along, the door is to pass through.

"I am the life" (14:6). Life is not something apart from us; life is what we truly are.

I am the truth" (14:6). Truth is not something that remains outside, but that which opens (*aletheia*) our mind.

"I am the good shepherd" (10:11). The good shepherd is not the one who stands apart, but the one who lets his life merge into that of the sheep.

"I am the vinestock" (15:5). The vine-stock is not separate from the branches, but the source and subject of their life.

With these symbols Jesus made it clear to us that he is not just a person of the historical past, but the divine presence here and now. Christ is Immanuel, God with us. Through Jesus Prayer we wake to the inner presence of Christ. This mystical experience of Christ in us is the goal of Jesus Prayer. In deep mystical consciousness God is not just a *thou* before us, but the Self, the Spirit, within us. Paul experienced the depth of this consciousness and cried out: I live, not I; Christ lives in me (Gal.2:20), Christ is life for me (Phil 1:21). He experienced Christ as the true Self of his being. The Spirit revealed in Christ is the true subject of our being. This is the ultimate experience of Jesus Prayer: "We are called to have a share in the divine nature" (II. Pet. 1:4).

Christ-Consciousness in Paul

Paul consistently emphasises this mystical dimension of our relationship with Christ: "Everyone who is joined to the Lord is one Spirit with him" (I Cor. 6:17). Our true life merges with the life of Christ in us. Faith is insertion to divine life through Christ. In faith we recognize:

our life is hidden in Christ.(Col.3:3),

we are reborn in Christ (II Cor.5:17),

we grow into maturity in Christ (Eph. 3:16),

we are clothed in Christ (Gal. 3:27),

we are being transformed into the image of Christ (II Cor. 3:18),

we reflect the glory of Christ (II Cor. 3:18)

we live the life of Christ (Gal. 2:20)

we mature into the fullness of Christ (Eph. 4:13)

we are being renewed in Christ (Gal.6:15)

Christ is in us (Rom.8:10)

we are in Christ (Eph. 1:4)

Christ is our life (Phil. 1:20, Rom. 6:23)

Christ is our light (II Cor. 4:6)

Christ is our freedom (II Cor.3:17, Gal. 5:1, Rom. 8:2)

we are the heirs of God, co-heirs of Christ (Rom.8:17)

we are the limbs of the body of Christ (I Cor. 12:27)

Christ is the fulfilment of our life (Col. 2:10)

In the deepest experience of Christ-consciousness we should be able to cry out with Paul: "I live, not I, Christ lives in me" (Gal.2:20). To believe in Christ means not just relating us to Jesus as the historical person of the past, but inserting us to the present reality of the living

Christ. Christ is God with us, God within us, God all-in-all. The Letter to the Ephesians describes unto what experience this Christ consciousness finally leads us: "to be filled with the utter fullness of God" (3:19).

Theosis in Church Fathers

The early Church Fathers used poetic symbols to clarify the divinisation process taking place within us. (PG = *Patrologia Graeca*; PL = *Patrologia Latina*)

"God became man so that man may become God! (*Deus homo factus est, ut homo fieret Deus*) (Augustine, *PL.38, 1997*).

"Through his immense love the Word of God became what we are, so that we may become perfectly what he is" (Irenaeus, *PG. 7,1120*).

"There is a divine seed in man: man becomes not God, but is being divinized" (Clement of Alexandria, *Stromata, 7.10.57*)

"When our consciousness is completely purified and through contemplation elevated above the material realm, it will be divinised by God" (Origen, *Comm. on John´s* Gospel, 32,27).

"The Word of God became man, so that we humans may become divine" (Athanasius, *PG. 25, 192*) "In the Spirit the Word divinizes us" (Athanasius, *PG 26, 589*).

"In the Holy Spirit the divine Word divinizes us" (Origen, *PG. 26, 589*)

"With Jesus human and divine natures begin to be woven together so that by fellowship with divinity human nature might become divine, not only in Jesus, but also in all those who believe and go on to undertake the life which Jesus taught" (Origen, *Contra Celsum*, 3,28).

"We have not only become Christians, but Christ himself. Stand firm in awe and rejoice: we have become Christ" (Augustine, *Commentary on John´s Gospel, 21,8*)

"The Word became man, so that we humans may become Divine. Theosis means the re-forming of the Image of God according to which we have been created by the Word" (Athanasius, *De Incarnatione 3,101*).

"In the Spirit the Word divinises us" (Athanasius, *PG.25, 192; 26,589*).

"Christ is Son by nature; we are sons by grace" (Athanasius, *PG. 26, 361c*)

"Christ takes shape in us through the Holy Spirit who reinstates the divinity in us" (Cyril of Alexandria, *PG.75,1088*).

"Theosis is participation through grace in the nature of God" (John of Damascus, *Expositio Fidei, 88,18*).

"Through theosis we are brought into the energy-field of God" (Gregory Palamas, *Holy Hesychasm*). Gregory Palamas explains theosis with the symbol of the sun: what is our relationship with the sun? On the one hand, the sun is far away, an unattainable reality and incomprehensible mystery. On the other hand, the sun shines through us for every cell of the body is energized by the sun; we live and through the sun: the sun is transcendent and immanent; so is the Divine transcendent and immanent. We live the divine life. "Divinisation is not immersion into the essence of the Divine, but transformation through the energies of the Divine. These energies are felt in the purified soul" (*Holy Hesychasm*).

"The only begotten Son of God, wanting to make us sharers in his divinity, assumed our nature, so that he, made man, might make us gods" (Thomas Aquinas, *Opus*, 57, 1-4).

Divinisation in Christian Mystics

Mystics try to describe this experience with poetic imageries:

I am a branch of the divine vine-stock (John 15:5),

> I am a fountain of the divine waters (John 7:37),
>
> I am a part of the divine body (I Cor. 12,12),
>
> I am a son/daughter of God (Rom 8:16),
>
> I am an heir of God, co-heir with Christ. (Rom. 8:17),
>
> God gives birth to himself in me (Origen),
>
> I am the mother God (Gregory of Nyssa),
>
> I am ray of the divine sun (Hyppolitus),
>
> I am a spark of the divine Light (Meister Eckhart),
>
> I give birth to the One who gives birth to me (Meister Eckhart),
>
> I am a drop / wave of the divine ocean (Theresa of Avila),
>
> I am a flame of the divine fire (John of the Cross).

These expressions cannot be grasped by human efforts, nor understood by the reasoning process of the mind. The mystics demand that we open ourselves to the intuitive movements of the nous/buddhi and perceive divinisation in the heart. The entry into this inner divine space is a gift of the grace. When we are graced with this enlightenment, we realize the divine core of our being, the divine dimension of our true self within. Human consciousness is transformed, deepened and integrated with the divine consciousness. The Divine in the human wakes up. The Divine unfolds itself through the human. Then we may be able to exclaim: *I am divine!*[2]

Mercy as the Fruit of Divinisation

What does this experience mean for our life? This experience supplies our life a divine axis. All that we do comes from this divine consciousness at the core of our being. Then our activities get a divine horizon, a divine dimension, a divine meaning. They become truly participation in the divine work of renewing this world; we become instruments in the hands of the divine Spirit. God works through us. Then we are able to make decisions with a deeper consciousness, not just to satisfy the greed of the ego or to please the constraints of the world, but to respond to the Spirit within. We can thus discern God's will in our decision-making process. The inner light shines through and enlightens our path.

What would be the concrete effect of divinisation in human life? Through this experience a transference of the centre of the person takes place: from the ego-centredness to God-centredness, from *aham-kāra* to *ātma-bōdha*. "I move out of the centre of my life and God moves in" (Meister Eckhart, *Et cum factus esset..*). The one who lives from a divine centre of life, will be a person endowed with mercy. The face of God manifest in Jesus has been the merciful face of God. In the lives of the poor and on the faces of the broken humans one discovers the healing presence of the God who creates everything new. Mercy is not what we produce as sympathy, but what we receive from the inner divine fountain. The divine love as mercy flows through our heart into the world. We become channels of the divine mercy. This is a birthing process: we are born of God in divinisation and we give birth to God through mercy. Through our merciful dealings, the divine mercy touches the hearts of people and transforms their life. We are not only children of God, but mothers of God. "The soul gives birth to Christ through good works" (Origen, *On the Gospel of John, 32, 27*). "What once happened in a bodily way in Mary continues to happen in every soul that lives according to the Logos. Thus everyone can become the mother of God" (Gregory of Nyssa, *On the Gospel of Mathew, 12,50*). "I give birth to Him of whom I am born" (Meister Eckhart, *Ave gratia plena*).

Endnotes

[1] Lev Gillet (1987), p. 27.

[2] S. Painadath SJ (2018).

7

Spirituality of Jesus Prayer

We have looked at the structure of the inner spiritual journey into the realm of the heart. We have then explored how Jesus went on this inner journey, what divine consciousness he had, and what he wanted to communicate to us.

Now we shall see how the practice of Jesus Prayer helps us to enter into this experience. What is important is to move down from the upper level of the mental perception to the deeper levels of the contemplative awareness, from mind to the nous.

In order to silence the mind it is recommended to repeat a key word or phrase, a mantra or the name of the divine Lord. This is being practiced in most cultures and religions all over the world. The mind always looks for something new and dynamic; repetition is not something that the mind likes. Hence the mind drops that which is being repeated. In this way the mental activity is brought to stillness; the mind becomes serene.

In Jesus Prayer three elements are used in this process of repetition: breathing, mantra and the divine name.

Breathing

Breathing is not just a biological activity of sustaining life. Through breathing we imbibe the cosmic energy of life that ultimately comes forth from a divine source. "God breathed the breath of life into the nostrils of Adam and gave him life" (Gen.2:7). The Creator continues to breathe into creation. We read in the Bible: "It is God's breath that made me, and keeps me alive" (Job, 33:4). "If God were to take back his breath from our nostrils, we all will return to dust" (Job, 34:15). "If you stop their breath they die and revert to dust; if you give out your breath fresh life begins; you keep renewing the world" (Ps. 104). "It is God who gives life and breath to all beings" (Acts. 17:25). "Everything has its origin and sustenance in the breath of God" (Atharva Veda, 11.4.1) "Breath is divine" (Chandogya Up. 4.10.4). When we pay attention to the process of breathing with gratitude and respect, we become aware of the divine life-energy flowing through us. Attentiveness on the flow of breath puts the restless mind to rest. Nikephoros says, "Breathing is a natural way to the heart. In order to bring the mind to the heart, concentrate on the breath, and repeat the name of Jesus"[1] "If you truly wish to keep silence as you should and to be sober in your heart without effort, let the Jesus Prayer cleave to your breath and in a few days you will see it in practice" (Hesychius)[2]

Mantra

The second element is Mantra. Mantra is not a name, not a word, which has a conceptual meaning, but a sound, which creates vibrations in the inner realm, and thus deepens the consciousness. Through the repetition of the classical mantras, we tune ourselves to the cosmic symphony of life. We realise that we are part of the cosmic-divine web. The primordial mantra is OM. It consists of three syllables: A. U. and M. A = the beginning, U= the middle M= the end. AUM is pronounced as OM (Mandukya Up. 8). OM therefore signifies the totality of reality. Hence it is the sound symbol of the dynamic divine presence. OM is the divine sound that vibrates in everything. When we chant OM in a meditative mood the mind sinks into the nous, consciousness is deepened, and one is attuned to the divine vibration within oneself and in the cosmos.

The Name

The third element is the name of the divine Lord. In each religion the devotees chant that name which is most sacred to them. (eg. Hinduism: Siva or Rama, Buddhism: Buddha, Islam: 99 names of Allah). For us Christians the name of Jesus Christ communicates intensely the transforming power and presence of God. It is in and through Jesus that we have recognised the face of God turned in mercy towards the world; hence this is the name most dear to us. There are two ways of understanding the role of the name of Jesus in prayer: In the Latin West, the name only signifies the person and presence of Christ. In the Greek East, the name contains the presence and hence a devout repetition of the name gives the experience of the real presence and power of Christ. It is like the difference between an image of Jesus and the Eucharistic host that contains the real presence. It is in the latter sense that the practice of Jesus Prayer flourished in the East. "The ascetics of the East testify that the name has in it God´s power and presence: not only is God invoked by this name, he is already present in the invocation"[3] While praying the name of Jesus with attentiveness and self-surrender, we wake to the real presence of Christ within our heart. Jesus Prayer can thus be a sacramental experience. John Chrysostom, one of the great Fathers of the Eastern Church said on this: "Remain in the devout repetition of the name of Jesus Christ, so that the heart absorbs the divine Lord and the Lord captures the heart; both become one" (*PG. 60, 75*).

Practising the Name

The practice of praying the name of Jesus started with the Desert Fathers in Egypt and it continued in the Greek Church. At the beginning only the name *Jesus* was being repeated. Later came up formulas like:

Lord Jesus,

Lord Jesus, have mercy on me,

Lord Jesus, Son of God, have mercy on me,

Jesus Christ, Son of God, have mercy on me, a sinner.

The Greek expression *Kyrie eleison, Christe eleison,* has a rhythm and vibration that bring the mind to inner concentration. This is important in selecting the formula. Our heart should resonate with the formula. All spiritual masters insist that the name *Jesus* should be included in the formula. The repetition of the divine name of Jesus would then evoke vibrations in the inner realm and lead to a deep oneness-experience.

Practicing Jesus Prayer is like a bird soaring high into the skies. The bird needs quite a lot of effort to fly to the heights; it has to flap its wings and struggle to soar high. This is like the first stage of Jesus Prayer, where one needs to sit calmly, control the wandering mind, get the psychic movements focused, come to an interior silence and then repeat the name of *Jesus* for a long period of time.

Once the bird has attained a certain altitude it can just glide in the air without much exertion. It floats serenely in the air. Similarly in the second stage of Jesus Prayer the repetition continues without much effort. After some time we feel as if we do not repeat the name, it repeats itself. We are just aware of the name being repeated from within. The mind becomes calm and serene. No more exertion is needed; repetition takes place deep in us. We just sit quietly and become aware of the power of the name of Jesus that enables us to relish the presence of the Lord within us. The human soul soars to the heights of spiritual experience.

For the Desert Fathers two things are important in the practice of Jesus Prayer: (i). As a river flows quietly, without interruption, should one practice the repetition of the name: with the same speed, same rhythm and same serenity. (ii). Keep the mind empty of thoughts, steady, fixed on Christ in you, serene, joyful, peaceful. Whatever distracting thoughts come up, surrender them all to the inner divine Master. Do not get disturbed. The essence of Jesus Prayer is to be established in the remembrance of God and to live in his presence. The unceasing invocation of the divine name will keep the mind on the single thought of God and in communion with him.

According to Kallistos Ware, there are three levels in the practice of Jesus Prayer: "It starts as *prayer of the lips*: oral prayer; then it grows more inward, becoming *prayer of the mind*: mental prayer. Finally the mind descends into the heart and is united with it, and so the prayer becomes *prayer of the heart*, or prayer of the nous in the heart…The ultimate purpose of the spiritual way is not just a person who says prayers from time to time, but a person who is prayer all the time: a state of prayer that is unceasing, which continues uninterrupted even in the midst of other activities."[4]

Prayer in Daily Life

Invocation of the name of Jesus is a simple form of prayer. Seekers of all age groups, young and old, of any profession, can use this form effectively. And this can be practiced at every moment of our daily life. While working in the garden or in the kitchen, while dressing or walking, travelling or relaxing, at moments of distress or mental strain, Jesus Prayer can be practiced. Though it began as a prayer for monks and hermits, it is equally a prayer form for a person leading family or professional life in the world. Kallistos and Ignatius Xantopoulos, Byzantine spiritual masters (14-15 century) quote John Chrysostom: "Whether one eats or drinks, sits or serves, travels or does anything else, must unceasingly cry out Jesus Prayer. In this way the name of the Lord will descent into the depth of the heart, so that the heart may absorb the Lord and the Lord absorbs the heart, and the two become one. Do not severe your heart from God, but dwell with him until the name of the Lord is deeply rooted there and you cease to think of anything else".[5]

The name of Jesus penetrates the soul just as a drop of oil seeps through the wick of a lamp bringing forth a bright flame. Through Jesus Prayer one can attain inner peace, bliss and deep spiritual experiences. There is no special place or time bound with it. But the spiritual masters insist that in the beginning it is important that we devote a certain amount of time for a disciplined daily exercise of praying in this form. For this we must find a quiet time and a serene place. All thoughts and feelings which surface during the exercise must be brought to the name of Jesus and surrendered to the divine Lord. There is no need to be disturbed about distractions. Every bit of tension and haste must be avoided. "You should not make long prayers, for it is better to pray little but often. Superfluous words are idle talk" (St. Theophylact, *Commentary on the Gospel of Mathew*, 6,7).[6] After every invocation of the name a moment of contemplative silence could be inserted to deepen the awareness. If fatigue comes upon, the invocation could be interrupted and taken up again later. The goal is not a constant literal repetition, but attentiveness to the indwelling presence of Christ in the heart. Attentiveness to this presence is far more important than any feeling of devotion. "I sleep, but my heart keeps awake" (Song of Songs). The essence of Jesus Prayer is the constant interior attentiveness to the indwelling presence of the Risen Christ within the heart. Being in his presence is the core of Jesus Prayer. Hence it is called the inner spiritual prayer. The vocal repetition is only a preparation for the inner spiritual prayer. Repeating the name without inner attentiveness is like trying to ignite the wood without fire. In the course of time we may come to a phase wherein the prayer remains with us throughout the day and night.

Three Phases of Jesus Prayer

1. Active Phase (Mind). In an atmosphere of peace and serenity one sits quietly, in the mood of adoration, surrendering all thoughts and desires at the feet of the divine Master. Realise that one sits in the presence of the Divine: concentrate on the presence of the Lord within. With devotion and love invoke the name of Jesus. Repeat the name with a certain inner rhythm that evokes spiritual vibrations; there is no need to think on the name. After some time boredom may be felt, a dryness and frustration, a feeling that one is not gaining anything. A lot of distracting thoughts may hit like waves on the shore of the mind. In such moments one should not stop repeating the name. In fact the mind is being purified through these torments.

We have to pass through this phase of inner purification. Classical spiritual masters speak of the *purgative way* that can last for days and months. One may feel cold, arid, lost and sterile. Here we are led through a desert of inner dryness, which is a process of getting rid of inordinate attachments. The divine Spirit is leading us to fresh well-springs through this desert experience. Hold on! This is like a pilot dealing with the aeroplane when confronted with turbulence; with intensified attention he steers the plane to safety. Inner disturbances are an invitation to put renewed trust in God´s abiding presence, in the inner guidance of the Spirit, and continue to repeat the name faithfully and devoutly. In order to purify the mind and attain concentration we need to go through this turbulence experience, the *dark night of the soul.* During this time of darkness, the desert experience, we actually grow deeper. In fact God reveals himself through the veil of interior darkness. (Job 38, 17-19). "Every time thoughts begin to confuse you, you have only to descend into the heart and the thoughts will flee."[7]

We should faithfully and with devotion hold on to the divine name. "The name of Jesus is itself an instrument of purification, a filter through which pass only thoughts, words and acts, compatible with the Christ-consciousness. The growth of the name in the heart implies a corresponding death to the ego-self, from which all sins comes forth."[8] Gradually mind becomes serene and focussed on the divine Master within.

2. Receptive Phase (Nous). Slowly the process gets more interiorised. After the initial phase of constant repetition a phase comes where the repetition stops spontaneously; the name is being repeated from within. I do not repeat, it repeats. Now the name of Jesus is being repeated in the deeper realms of the nous. It is being remembered within. One becomes more receptive at this moment. Distracting words and images become less and they disappear; just the name of Jesus lingers on. Thoughts and feelings merge into the power of the name. Through the grace of the Spirit one begins to experience the divine presence within: stillness, peace, joy and the sweetness of the name of Jesus.

3.Contemplative Phase. (Heart). The name penetrates the deeper recess of the heart. Mind sinks into deep mystical silence. Only a sense of the divine presence is felt. The soul becomes silent, serene and receptive. The Holy Spirit takes possession of the human soul fully. My soul and the divine Spirit merge into one. This is the deep experience of mystical union. The soul merges into a deep divine silence. "The one who holds on the Lord, becomes one Spirit with the Lord" (I Cor. 6, 17). The soul no more feels an existence separate from the Divine. This is the consciousness of the process of divinisation that is taking place deep within us. The human soul is being charged with divine energies. Just as a piece of iron in the furnace glows with the power of the fire, just as a lens transmits fully the sun light, just as the branches of the vine-stock are totally transparent to the vital sap of the trunk, the soul becomes a transparent medium of the divine light and life, power and presence. God shines through the soul. Here the quest of the soul for God gets fulfilled at least for a few moments. It is a contemplative perception of one´s being soaked in the divine presence: being silent to the divine silence.

In this experience there is no name, no form of God: all concepts, images and symbols of God are left outside. One finds oneself within `the cave of the heart´, within `the interior castle´ of the soul. This is an intense experience of divine grace. We do not attain it through our efforts. All that we can do is to open ourselves to the divine presence through Jesus Prayer. Genuine God-experience is ultimately a gift of grace. All the inner faculties of human perception - senses, mind, psyche and buddhi – come to an inner resonance. One gets into harmony with the entire universe of persons and things. This is hesychia.

Prayer of the Mystery

The Prayer of the name of Jesus is not just a means to a deeper prayer, but it leads us to the ultimate goal of prayer: Christ-consciousness, experiencing the transforming presence of the Spirit within. Hence it is important to repeat the name of Jesus with affection and surrender, with an ineffable awareness of the inner divine presence. With a sense of being confronted by the mystery of the Divine, the soul would become aware of its smallness, its unworthiness, its shadows and sinfulness. It is with this genuine humility that the prayer comes: *Lord Jesus Christ have mercy on me a sinner*. One does not have to create unnecessary guilt feelings. It is rather the awakening of the creature to the greatness of the Creator: adoration at the heart of the cosmos. Jesus Prayer vibrates at the heart of the universe. Attentiveness (*nipsis*) to this presence is far more important than any feeling of devotion.

In *The Centuries*, a classical book on Jesus Prayer, we read:

> "The name of Jesus comes into our life first of all as a lamp in the darkness, next it is like moonlight and finally like the sunrise. Being the sun of our intellect it creates within it luminous thoughts to which it communicates its own splendour, thoughts resembling the sun. It is love which elevates us – we should notice the part played by divine love in this process of transformation and makes us higher than angels. To pronounce the name of Jesus in a holy way is an all surpassing aim for human life. Truly blessed is he who unceasingly pronounces in his heart the name of Jesus, and who in the depths of his mind is united to the Jesus Prayer as the body to the surrounding air, and as wax to the flame." (*The Centuries*, ch. 2. 69-94)[9]

Endnotes

[1] cit. *Writings from the Philokalia* (1995), p. 33.

[2] cit. *Writings from the Philokalia* (1995), p. 194.

[3] Gillet (1987), p. 84.

[4] Ware (1979), p. 165.

[5] cit. *Writings from the Philokalia* (1995), p. 193.

[6] cit. Chariton (1996). p. 50.

[7] (Theophan) cit. Chariton (1996), p. 184.

[8] Gillet (1987), p. 96.

[9] cit. Gillet (1987), pp. 40-41.

Theology of Jesus Prayer

In the previous chapters we dwelt on the process of divinisation and how Jesus Prayer leads to this mystical experience. Now we shall reflect theologically on some of the basic elements of the practice of Jesus Prayer.

Hesychia

The Eastern Fathers and the Masters of Jesus Prayer speak of hesychia as the core element of the theology of Jesus Prayer. It is the classical term for the deepest inner experience of Jesus Prayer. The Greek word *hesychia* means repose, tranquillity, solitude, withdrawal into the inner divine silence. It is withdrawal from the turbulent field of the exterior senses and from the hectic activities of the mind, withdrawal into the nous, the intuitive faculty, and through the nous entry into the heart. One waits upon God in quietness and silence, no longer talking about or to God, but simply listening. "Be still and know that I am God" (Ps. 46:10).

Hesychia is an experience of a deeper consciousness, where we are actually true to our real self. Within the heart we realise who we really are, and who God is. Within the heart one is alone with God. It is an experience of immediacy, in the sense that there is no mediating being between the soul and God. It is the experience of deep divine silence graced by the Spirit. When one wakes to the inner cave of the heart, one sits in deep silence in the divine presence. No chanting, no prayer! The thoughts and words, emotions and desires – all become silent in the divine presence. The sense of the ego too disappears and only the pure presence is experienced. Deep within, one experiences inner peace, inner bliss. This is hesychia: access to the deep experience of mystical union. Here we realise that *we are divine*, that God is the true subject of our being. One experiences oneself to be just an instrument in the hands of God, just a channel that transmits his presence. Even if the surroundings are noisy and turbulent, they do not disturb us, for we have an abiding experience of the inner presence of the Divine.

When we pray to God in thoughts and words, we imagine God before us as a personal thou. But in the contemplative solitude of the hesychia we realise that we are in the Divine, that the Divine is in us, that we are ultimately ONE with the Divine. Jesus Prayer is a hesychast prayer. At the beginning of the recitation it may look as if we are praying to Jesus out there, invoking a God before us. But soon the consciousness sinks deeper than the mental realm and moves towards the nous. For this mystical immersion, the repetition of the name of Jesus is extremely helpful and powerful. One just sits in divine presence without expressly doing anything, or praying for anything. All the inner faculties get focused on Christ within. Everything becomes silent and serene. Is this not what Jesus meant when he said, "the Kingdom of God is within you"? In Indian heritage this is the experience of *Ātmabōdha* (Self-realisation): know who you are, *you are divine!*

There are two degrees of hesychia: "In the first degree the soul sees everything and is conscious of itself and of its external surroundings. It can reason and govern itself" (Theophan)[1] The second degree of hesychia is called ecstasy or ravishment. St. Issac the Syrian explains it in this way: "The Spirit of prayer comes upon the soul and carries it into such a state of contemplation that the soul is no more aware of the external surroundings, ceases to reason and only contemplates. It has no power to control itself, or to break away from this state. It is said that Seraphim of Sarov (1759-1833) began to pray before his evening meal and came to himself only next morning. This is the prayer of ravishment. With some this has been accompanied by illumination of their faces. A number of Eastern saints experienced a share in the mystery of Our Lord's Transfiguration; their face or entire body was surrounded and illuminated with divine light"

(Theophan).[2] "See to it that the light inside you is not darkness. If your whole body is filled with light, it will be lighted up entirely, as when the lamp shines on you with its rays" (Lk. 11:35-36). Prayer in such a person is no longer a series of acts, rather it is a dynamic state, where the Spirit takes possession of a person; one does not cease to pray because the Spirit constantly prays in oneself. This is the meaning of *unceasing prayer* (I Thess. 5:16).

Hesychasm insists on individual sanctification in solitude. John Climacus, the classical spiritual master and author of *The Ladder*, exhorts: "Repeat the name of Jesus with your breathing and you will know the power of hesychia" (*Ladder 27*).Through the attentive and devotional repetition of the name of Jesus the mind is anchored in the nous, and gradually through the nous one enters the inner divine realm of the heart. Nicetas Stethatos, the biographer of Symeon the New Theologian, says: "Man´s return to the original divine image demands a reshaping of our senses and their reordering once more under the guidance of the nous. The external senses should receive only the logoi (essential impressions of things); they must be dematerialised and should render the irrational submissive to that which is intelligible. We are brought back from carnal satisfaction to higher ends. This is the purpose of asceticism."[3] "Once the mind is thus united with the heart, one discovers the treasure hidden in the field, the pearl beyond price" (Theophan).[4] From Isaac the Syrian Monk and spiritual teacher of hesychia we hear: "Enter eagerly into the treasure-house that is within you and so you will see the treasure-house of heaven."[5]

Christ-Consciousness

What is the treasure, the imperishable pearl that we are discovering in hesychia? It is the experience of the presence of Christ within us. Jesus experienced God as the true subject of his being, as the root of his being, as the hidden fountain within him, as the source of his being, as *that out of which* he came forth. And Jesus wanted to communicate this experience to us. We are called to experience God as the subject within us. The divine subject in us is Christ. "I live, not I, Christ lives in me", says St. Paul expressing the core of Christian spirituality (Gal.2:20). Christ is Immanuel, God-with-us, God-within-us. The focus of our faith is not just the historical person Jesus of Nazareth, who lived 2000 years ago, but the risen Christ, who is alive today with-us, within-us. "For me life is Christ", says Paul (Phil.1:21). God within us - this is Christ in the Christian faith experience. Our life evolves in Christ; our life unfolds from Christ. The entire theology of Paul can be summarised in one mantra: *in Christ*; he uses this term 144 times in his Letters.

When through the repetition of the name of Jesus our consciousness sinks into the heart, we realise that Christ is the true divine subject of our being: we sink into Christ, we get immersed into Christ, we grow into Christ, we are inserted to Christ, we live in Christ, we are transformed unto Christ - these are the images which Paul uses profusely to describe our relation to Christ. We meet Jesus Christ not before us, but within us, not in yesterday, but in today, not by turning the pages of history into the foregone past, but by opening ourselves to the divine depth of the present moment. This is what Jesus meant when he said: "abide in me, and I abide in you" (Jn. 15: 5). "Just as the Father is in me and I am in the Father, so I am in you and you are in me" (Jn. 17:21-23).

Christ-consciousness means the inner awakening to this indwelling presence of Christ; this is the fruit of Jesus Prayer. St. Nikephoros, Monk of Athos, (14 cent.) teaches: "We are to call to mind Jesus Christ until the name of the Lord penetrates our heart, descends to its very depths, crushes the dragon and gives life to the soul. Our heart is to absorb the Lord, and the Lord to absorb our heart, and the two are to become one. The name of Jesus, once it has become the centre of our life, brings everything together."[6]

With this experience we can live differently in the world, in the midst of all sorts of activities. We live from within the divine silence and rootedness. We live in Christ; Christ lives in us. The divine Spirit transforms our life constantly into the New Life in Christ. This is not running away from the world of activities, but a deeper insertion into the milieu of activities and responsibilities. We become more effective instruments in the hand of God.

The Holy Spirit in us

For the great masters of Jesus Prayer, the experience of Christ within us, is the experience of the Holy Spirit. Ultimately there is no difference between these two dimensions of mystical experience, for "the risen Lord has become the life-giving Spirit" (II Cor. 3:17). "When the Spirit of God descends upon a person and overshadows him with the fullness of his outpouring, the soul overflows with indescribable joy, for the Holy Spirit turns to joy whatever he touches" (St Seraphim of Sarov). [7]

Jesus experienced the Spirit as the divine energy within himself. It is in the Spirit that the Logos became flesh (Lk. 1:35), it is in the Spirit that Jesus grew up in wisdom, it is the Spirit that anointed Jesus at the baptism in Jordan (Lk. 3:22), it is the Spirit that led him to the desert (Lk. 4:1) and brought him to public life (Lk. 4:14). At the very outset of his public ministry Jesus proclaimed: "The Spirit of the Lord is upon me; he has anointed me and sent me to bring Good News to the poor.(Lk. 4:18). It is with the power of the divine Spirit that Jesus spoke (Lk. 10:21) worked miracles, (Mt. 12:28) healed the sick (Mk. 5:30) and opposed the powers of evil (Mt. 12:28). It is the Spirit that continues his salvific work in the world (Jn. 14:26) and brings everything to fulfilment (Rom. 8:23). To live in Christ means to live in the Spirit. To grow in Christ means to grow in the Spirit. Freedom in Christ means freedom in the Spirit (Gal. 5:16). It is the Spirit that makes us realise that we are children of God, heirs of God and co-heirs of Christ (Rom. 8:17).

Holy Spirit in Prayer

The Holy Spirit within us is the true subject of prayer. "We do not know how to pray in the right way; the Spirit helps us in our weakness and prays from within us in a way that cannot be put into words" (Rom. 8:26). The God, to whom we pray, is actually the God who prays from within us: God-as-Spirit. The Spirit is therefore the true subject of prayer.

This becomes very clear in the case of Jesus Prayer. "We do not choose the Prayer of Jesus, we are led to it by the Spirit. The Spirit writes the name of Jesus in fiery letters upon our hearts. The name is a burning flame within us."[8] It is the Holy Spirit that breathes and groans in us, the Spirit that calls out *abba, Father*, the Spirit that speaks out incessantly the name of Jesus.

"No one can say, Jesus is the Lord, except in the Holy Spirit" (I Cor. 12:3). The name of Jesus is the articulation of the divine silence, the mantra that the divine Spirit murmurs incessantly within us. And when we repeat the name, we tune ourselves to this inner prayer of the Spirit. When we chant the name of Jesus, we resonate with the Spirit chanting within us.

This becomes very perceptible when we combine the name of Jesus with OM. OM is the divine sound, the vibration of the divine Logos, the resonance of the divine Spirit. When we chant *Jesu....OM....Jesu,* or *OM Jesu Christāya namah,* we can intensely feel that our entire being, body and soul, resonates with the divine vibrations.

The Divinisation

What is the grace of Jesus Prayer? It is the realisation of the divinisation (*theosis*) within and all around us. When the mind is settled in the heart through the nous, when the heart is attuned to the divine Spirit through the chanting of the name of Jesus, our consciousness wakes to the realisation of what is happening deep within us: the transformation of our being to the Divine, the divinisation of the human.

Origen clarifies this: "When our consciousness is purified and elevated above the sense level, it is divinised" (*PG. 14, 817a*).

Cyril of Alexandria says on this: "Christ takes shape in us through the Holy Spirit, who reinstates the divinity in us" (*PG. 75, 1088*).

Athanasius emphasises: "God is outside all things according to his essence, but in all things through his acts of power."[9]

St Basil affirms: "No one has ever seen the essence of God, but we believe in the essence, because we experience the energy". [10]

Augustine is quite clear on the divinisation: "God became human, so that we humans become divine" (*PL. 38.1997*).

The early Fathers called this transformation process *Theosis*, divinisation of the human. The invocation of the name of Jesus communicates the experience of divinisation.

Gregory Palamas (1296-1359), who is considered to be the spiritual master of divinisation in the Greek Church, explained how through Jesus Prayer one wakes to the divinisation process. The Divine as the transcendent reality is absolute mystery and unapproachable light. As creatures we do not participate in the divine *essence*. But the Divine as immanence, dwells in us through the divine Spirit, works in us through the divine *energies* and makes our being translucent through the divine Light. The divine energies consist in grace, life and power. "The divinisation is not immersion into the essence of the Divine, but transformation through the energies of the Divine. These energies are felt in the purified soul" (*Holy Hesychasm*). Jesus Prayer is an effective means of the purification and elevation of consciousness. Through Jesus Prayer one attunes oneself to the divinisation process. "We are in God, since we are deified by him, and God in us since it is he who deifies us" (*Topics of Natural and Theological Science* § 105).[11] Jesus Prayer makes us realise that our life evolves in the energy field of the Divine. "The one who is united with Lord Jesus Christ is one Spirit with him" (I Cor. 6:17). The *Catechism of the Catholic Church* states: "The name of Jesus is at the heart of Christian prayer. Many Christians, such as St. Joan of Arc, died with the one word "Jesus" on their lips" (*Nr. 435*).

Endnotes

[1] cit. Chariton (1996) p. 65.

[2] cit. Chariton (1996), p. 66.

[3] cit. Gillet (1987), p. 75.

[4] cit. Chariton (1996), p. 198.

[5] cit. Chariton (1996), p. 164.

[6] cit. Gillet (1987), p. 50.

[7] cit. Ware (1979), p. 118.

[8] Gillet (1987), pp. 97, 103.

[9] cit. Ware (1979), p. 27.

[10] cit. Ware (1979), p. 27.

[11] cit. Canilang (2010), p. 237.

9

Mystical Characteristics of Jesus Prayer

We have dwelt on the spirituality and theology of Jesus Prayer. Now let us look at some of the basic characteristics of Jesus Prayer:

Prayer of the Heart: Jesus Prayer is also known as the Prayer of the Heart. "The entire attention has to be brought into the heart, which is the divine space at the core of our being" (Theophan).[1] It is in the cave of the heart that one experiences the living presence of the risen Christ. Genuine prayer evolves in the heart. This is why Jesus said: When you pray go into your inner room, close the door and pray to the Father in silence. (Mt. 6:19). "Descend from the head into the heart. When we pray with the mind, we never attain to an immediate and personal encounter with God. By the use of the brain one will at best know about God, but one will not know God, for there can be no direct knowledge of God without an exceedingly great love. Such love comes not from the brain alone, but from the heart. It is necessary for one to descend from the head into the heart, the inner room to experience God" (Hieromonk Kallistos).[2] Heart is the spiritual centre of one's being.

Inner Spiritual Prayer: The essence of Jesus Prayer is the awareness of the divine presence within: attentiveness to the indwelling presence of Christ; being in his presence is the core of Jesus Payer. Hence it is called the inner spiritual prayer. The indwelling presence within the heart is the *treasure* hidden in the field, the *pearl* beyond price. The vocal invocation of the divine name is a support to inner prayer; the words pronounced are merely a help and hence they are not essential. "In prayer the simplest rule is not to form an image of anything: gathering the mind within the heart, stand in the conviction that God is near. Images, however sacred they may be, retain the attention outside. The concentration of attention within the heart – this is the starting point for all true prayer." (Theophan)[3] "In order not to fall into illusion while praying the name of Jesus do not permit any visual concept, image or vision in the mind" (St. Nil Sorsky, a Russian ascetic, 1433-1508).[4]

Prayer of Loving Attention / Prayer of Simple Gaze: Jesus Prayer begins as a vocal prayer. The rhythmic repetition of a short phrase without images, ideas and thoughts, enables one to advance to the mystery of God, and the prayer becomes the prayer of loving attention or the prayer of simple gaze where the soul rests in God. "The state of contemplation is a captivity of the mind and of the entire vision by a spiritual object so overpowering that all outward things are forgotten, and wholly absent from the consciousness. The mind and consciousness become so completely immersed in the object contemplated that it is as though we no longer possess them" (Theophan).[5] Theophan terms this state of contemplation "prayer of ecstasy" or "prayer of ravishment". Gradually the prayer ceases to be the result of one´s own efforts and becomes the Self-acting prayer (= Spirit-created prayer) and becomes the prayer of Christ in oneself.

Contemplative Prayer: While practicing Jesus Prayer, one may be granted from time to time moments of rapture. It comes on the person unexpectedly as a free gift. The words of prayer spontaneously cease. One experiences an immediate sense of God´s presence. This may be only a brief graced moment, not a continuous state. In this deep spiritual silence and inner bliss the soul is totally immersed in God: God alone exists; the ego-sense disappears. The human soul merges with the Divine. It is the experience of a deeper spiritual union, spiritual bliss and joy. One enters the Kingdom of God within. Blessed Elisabeth of the Trinity said: "Heaven is God, and God is in my heart." In this hesychia experience attention descends into the heart; words and thoughts disappear; one feels a sort of warmth in the heart. It may consist only in being in God, in an opening of the heart to Him in reverence and love. It is a state of being irresistibly drawn within to stand in God in prayer. It is no longer we who pray, but it is the Spirit of God that prays in us. The Spirit that prays draws us to the depth of the heart. "The Spirit explores the depths of everything, even the depths of God." (I Cor. 2:10).

Prayer of Silence: True silence is a great gift of God. It is in silence and stillness that we experience God and feel his presence within. True silence is not merely an absence of noise, an external physical silence, although it is necessary at times, especially at the beginning. It is the outer and inner noise that prevents us from feeling God´s presence within. In order to arrive at true silence, we have to silence our mind. By the constant repetition of the name of Jesus, by the power of the name, mind gets purified and strips itself of distractions and attachments to external world and its allurements. The mind attaches itself and clings on to the sweetness of the name of Jesus and experiences the inner spiritual joy. This is contemplative silence. It is in this attentive and alert silence (*śraddhā*) that one experiences the Divine within the heart (*hesychia*).

Unceasing Prayer: The habit of Jesus Prayer is the easiest way of ascending into the unceasing prayer of the heart. Apart from the times of prayer, the utterance of the name of Jesus continues in the heart, of its own accord. While working in the garden or in the kitchen or in the office, while travelling, driving or walking, at all times Jesus Prayer can be practiced. One begins and ends the day with Jesus Prayer. The power of the divine name will penetrate the mind and the heart and continue silently within, without any conscious effort. Prayer becomes synchronized to the rhythm of breathing and the heart-beat. St. Paul exhorted the communities: "Be joyful always, pray at all times, be thankful in all circumstances. This is what God wants from you, in your life, in union with Christ Jesus." (I Thess. 5:16-18).

Constant Remembrance of God: The essence of Jesus Prayer is to be established in the remembrance of God and to live in his presence. The unceasing invocation of the divine name will keep the mind on the single thought of God and in communion with him. This is like cultivating a crop. We put the manure at the root, not on the branches, where the fruits emerge. The root absorbs the manure and transforms it to vital sap and as a result the tree bears flowers and fruits. So too in spiritual life: with the constant remembrance of Christ within we fertilise spiritual life. So we bear fruits in the Spirit. St. Dimitri of Rostov (1651-1709) says: "To kindle in his heart divine love, to unite with God in an inseparable union of love, it is necessary to pray often, raising the mind to God. As a flame increases when it is constantly fed, so prayer made often with the mind dwelling ever more deeply in God, arouses divine love in the heart, and the heart set on fire will warm all the inner man, will enlighten and teach him, revealing to him all its unknown and hidden wisdom, and making him like a flaming seraph always standing before God within his spirit, always looking at him within his mind and drawing from this vision the sweetness of spiritual joy".[6]

Burning of the Spirit: When the spark of God´s love, spark of grace, falls into the heart, the unceasing Jesus Prayer fans it into a flame. The more the divine name penetrates into the heart, the warmer the heart becomes and it inflames the soul with an inexpressible love towards God and humans and to the cosmos. "Unceasing prayer serves to maintain the inner fire, the burning of the Spirit" (John Chrysostom).[7] Through creation one rises to the Creator. "Sometimes I experienced a sweet burning in my heart, at other times a burning love for Jesus Christ and all of God´s creation. I felt a great joy in calling on the name of Jesus Christ and I realised the meaning of the words the Kingdom of God is within you (Lk. 17:21)" (*Way of a Pilgrim*).[8] Invocation of the name of Jesus as a vocal prayer begins with strenuous effort, but soon it flows on its own like a brook that murmurs in the heart. One will experience within oneself a small murmuring stream. This is a great blessing and brings about inner joy.

Spiritual Sobriety (*Nepsis*): *Nepsis* is a Greek word which means sobriety / attentiveness / wakefulness / watchfulness / vigilance / alertness / guarding the heart / *sraddha*. This is an indispensible condition for Jesus Prayer. Sobriety means total vigilant control of oneself for the purpose of keeping the mind on the single thought of God. In the *Method of Holy Prayer* of Symeon the New Theologian one reads: "Sobriety and prayer are united like soul and body. If one is lacking, the other cannot stand firm".[9] "The vision of God is granted to a person in proportion to his practice of what is pleasing to God: his avoidance of all that is not, his assiduity in prayer and the longing of his entire soul for God" (Gregory Palamas, *The Triads*).[10] This is spiritual sobriety, or *nepsis*.

Sobriety means to be present and alert in the present moment, where one is at this specific point in space and at this particular moment in time. Often we are scattered and dispersed, we are living with nostalgia for the past, or wishful thinking on the future. The neptic person understands the sacrament of the present moment: the person whom one meets here, the task in which one is engaged now – these are most important in one´s life at every given moment. Growing in sobriety means to acquire the power of discrimination, which enables one to discern the movements of the Spirit within and to disperse all irrelevant thoughts.

Engrafting the Divine Name in the Heart: The grafting of the name of Jesus in the heart takes place when one lives in the presence of God invoking the name as frequently as possible. Then one remembers God incessantly. This habit is not formed suddenly, but it requires long lasting discipline and perseverance. "Jesus Prayer becomes grafted in our heart: the hands at work, the mind and heart with God" (Theophan).[11] When one finds that the mind is getting distracted one could develop the habit of Jesus Prayer. John Climacus says: "God appears to the mind in the heart at first as a flame purifying its lover, and then as a light which illumines the mind and renders it God-like." (*The Ladder*)[12]

Endnotes

[1] cit. Chariton (1996), p. 17.

[2] cit. Chariton (1996), p.20.

[3] cit. Chariton (1996), p 183.

[4] cit. Chariton (1996), p 101.

[5] cit. Chariton (1996), p 23.

[6] cit. Chariton (1996), p 47.

[7] cit. Chariton (1996), p 151.

[8] *Way of a Pilgrim* (1978) pp. 40-41.

[9] cit. Gillet (1987), p. 75.

[10] cit. Canilang (2010), p. 211.

[11] cit. Chariton (1996), p 92.

[12] cit. *Writings from the Philokalia* (1995), p. 24.

10

Power of the Divine Name
in the New Testament

The original Hebrew form of the name *Jesus* is: Ye-ho-shua. It means "God saves", Yahweh is salvation. The name *Jesus* means Saviour

The Greek transcription of the Hebrew: Ie-schou-ah.

The Aramaic (Syriac) version for Jesus: Ii-śo   (iēe-śo)

The Latin version for Jesus: Jesus   (yē-sus)

The English term for Jesus: Jesus

In the New Testament the name of Jesus is mentioned in different forms:

Jesus of Nazareth: This is probably the most widely used name, Mk. 10:47, Mk. 14:67, Lk. 24:19. It was used to identify him on the Cross, Jn. 19:19.

Other frequently used titles include:

Jesus Son of David, Mk. 10:47.

Jesus the Galilean, Mk. 14:17

Greek speaking Christians from the beginning called Jesus *the Christos*, the anointed one.

For most of the Christian world the full name of Jesus is: Jesus Christ.

I.   The divine Name that came down from heaven

1.1   The divine *name Jesus* is revealed by the heavenly Father through the Holy Spirit to the Virgin Mary at the annunciation, Lk.1:30-32.

1.2 The holy *name Jesus* is revealed to Joseph by the angel of the Lord in a dream, Mt. 1:20-21.

1.3 The *name Jesus* is given to the baby at the time of circumcision, the name which was revealed by the angel to Joseph even before Jesus was conceived, Lk. 2:21.

1.4 The holy *name Jesus* is the name above all names, Phil. 2:9.

1.5 The entire creation bends the knee at the *name Jesus* and acclaims Jesus Christ as the Lord to the glory of God the Father, Phil.2:10-11.

1.6 By acknowledging the *name of Jesus* we offer God an unending sacrifice of praise, Heb. 13:15.

2. Praying in the name of Jesus

2.1 God the Father grants graces in the name of *Jesus*, Jn. 16:23.

2.2 Jesus invites us to ask the Father in *his name,* Jn. 16:24, 26.

2.3 Whenever we pray in the *name of Jesus*, we glorify the Father, Jn. 14:13.

2.4 God the Father will reward our prayer when we ask him in the *name of Jesus,* Jn. 15:16.

2.5 Always and in everything give thanks in the *name of Jesus,* the Lord, Eph. 5:20.

2.6 Jesus prayed to the Father to keep the chosen ones true to *his name,* Jn. 17:11.

2.7 The *name of Jesus* gives us the fullness of joy, Jn. 16:24.

2.8 Jesus keeps the chosen ones true to *his name,* Jn. 17:12.

2.9 Whatever you say or do, do it in the *name of Jesus* giving thanks to the Father through him, Col. 3:17.

3. Jesus's mission as the revelation of the name of the Father

3.1. Jesus understood that he came in the *name* of the Father, Jn. 5:43.

3.2   The *name of Jesus* is the manifestation of the work of the Father, Jn. 10:25.

3.3   Jesus understood his mission as making the *name of the Father* known to the world, Jn. 17:6.

3.4   Jesus made the *name of the Father* known to the disciples so that the love of the Father be in them, and Jesus will be in them, Jn. 17:26.

3.5   All who believe in the *name of Jesus* are given the grace to become the children of God, Jn. 1:12.

3.6   The Father sends the Spirit in the *name of Jesus,* Jn. 14:26.

3.7   Christ himself is present when we meet in *his name*, Mt. 18:20

4.   The name of Jesus saves us from sin and evil

4.1   The name *Jesus* overcomes the powers of evil, Lk.10:17.

4.2   In the name *Jesus* the disciples are empowered to overcome the powers of evil, Mk. 16:17.

4.3   Even those who do not belong to the community of the disciples, yet believe in the *name of Jesus*, are empowered to overcome the powers of evil by his name, Mk.9:38-39.

4.4   Signs and wonders are performed through the *name of Jesus*, Acts. 4:30.

4.5   Believing in the *name of Jesus* one has life eternal, Jn. 20:31.

4.6   The *name Jesus* saves the people from their sins, Mt. 1:21.

4.7   In the *name of Jesus* repentance for the forgiveness of sins will be preached to all peoples, Lk. 24:47.

4.8   Believers are justified in the *name of Jesus,* I Cor. 6:11.

4.9   Through the *name of Jesus* all sins will be forgiven, Acts. 10:43.

5. The healing power of the name of Jesus

5.1 In the *name of Jesus* Peter made the lame walk,   Acts. 3:6.

5.2 The faith in the *name of Jesus* grants healing and restores humans to health, Acts. 3:16.

5.3 The power of the *name of Jesus* is manifested in the healing, Acts. 9:34.

6. The name of Jesus and universal salvation

6.1 To believe in the *name of Jesus* is to believe in Jesus, the Son of God,   Jn. 3:18.

6.2 To believe in the *name of Jesus* is to have eternal life, I Jn. 5:13.

6.3 The divine commandment to believe in *the name of Jesus*, I. Jn. 3:23.

6.4 The *name of Jesus* has universal saving power, Acts. 4:12.

6.5 The disciples were asked not to teach in the *name of Jesus*, Acts. 4: 17

6.6 Jesus sends the disciples to go to all peoples and baptize them *into the name* of the Father and of the Son and of the Holy Spirit [The Latin Vulgate translation *in nomine* does not render the dynamic meaning of the Greek original *eis to onoma*, which would mean:initiate them *into* the life of the Father-Son-Spirit], Mt. 28:18.

6.7 Baptism in the *name of Jesus* brings about forgiveness of sins and gift of the Holy Spirit,   Acts. 2:38.

6.8 This man (Paul) is a chosen instrument to bring the name of Jesus before gentiles and kings and before the people of Israel, Acts 8:15

6.9 Believing in the *name of Jesus* they were baptised, Acts 8:12.

6.10 In the *name of Jesus* the peoples will put their hope, Mt. 12:21.

6.11   Condemnation for not believing in the *name of the Son,* Jn. 3:18.

7.   Persecutions in the name of Jesus

7.1   Jesus warned that his disciples will be hated by all on account of *his name,* but the man who stands firm will be saved, Mt. 10:22 ; Mt. 24:09 ; Mk. 13:13 ; Lk. 21:17 ; Lk. 21:12 ; Jn. 15:21.

7.2   Disciples were asked not to teach in the *name of Jesus,* Acts 5:28.

7.3   The disciples had the joy of suffering humiliation for the sake of the *name of Jesus,* Acts. 5:40-41.

7.4   I myself will show him (Paul) how much he must suffer for *my name,* Acts 8:16

7.5   One is blessed if one is reproached for the *name of Jesus,* I Pet. 4:14.

8.   The spiritual reward through the name of Jesus

8.1   Anyone who receives a little one in the *name of Jesus* receives Jesus himself and through him the Father, Mk.9:37 ; Mt. 18:5; Lk. 9:48.

8.2   Anyone who gives a cup of water in the *name of Jesus* will be rewarded, Mk. 9:41.

8.3   Anyone who renounces all possession for the *name of Jesus* will be repaid a hundred times over, and inherit eternal life, Mt. 19:29.

11
Spiritual Fruits of Jesus Prayer

Having seen the spirituality and theology of Jesus Prayer now we reflect on some of the fruits of Jesus Prayer that could deepen the God-experience and nourish our spiritual life.

I.   Experience of Christ in us

In the practice of Jesus Prayer attention is directed not to the historical Jesus who lived 2000 years ago, but to the Christ of the present moment: the risen Christ who lives in us, and in whom we live. We repeat the name of Jesus not turning back to the historical past, but waking up to the divine depth of the present moment. We wake to the salvific presence here and now, everywhere. Then Christ becomes for us the bread of life, the water of life, the way and light in the present.

2.   Christ-consciousness

The basic fruit of Jesus prayer is participation in the mystical self-consciousness – divine consciousness – of Jesus himself. Jesus lived out of the consciousness: I come forth from the Father, the Father has sent me, I live through the Father, I and the Father are ONE; I perform the works of the Father who dwells within me; I speak the words which are not my own but those of the Father in me. Jesus experienced the Divine as the subject of his being and mission. He was the manifestation of the Divine. Through Jesus Prayer we come to the experience that our life flows from Christ who dwells within, our life becomes a manifestation of Christ in us. Christ is the divine subject of our being, the true self within us. We realise that we are branches of the divine tree. Like branches we draw the vital sap (Spirit) from the root (Father) through the trunk (Christ), and produce flowers and fruits. We grow *into* the Father through Christ in the Spirit; we grow *out* of the Father through Christ in the Spirit.

With this we grow in the realisation that our life evolves within the inner-Trinitarian process.

3. Experience of the Indwelling Spirit

The Spirit of Christ transforms our life into divine life. Just as the sap of the tree flows constantly into the branches, the divine Spirit streams into our being through the prayer of the name of Jesus. The Spirit of Christ fills our being. Just as the sap is the nourishing source of the branches to produce flowers and fruits, the indwelling Spirit becomes the source of bearing fruits in our life. As we grow in Jesus Prayer, we enter into a receptive silence and we listen to the divine Spirit repeating the name from within our heart. We do not repeat the name, but the Spirit repeats it. This is what Paul meant when he said: "We do not know how to pray as we ought. In our weakness the Spirit comes to our help. The Spirit prays from our hearts in a way that cannot be expressed in words" (Rom. 8:26). The Spirit is the true subject of prayer. The God to whom we pray is the God who prays from within us.

4. Alertness to the Kingdom of God

Jesus came to proclaim the Kingdom of God. Kingdom means that God is at work in this world transforming everything to a new creation. Through the practice of Jesus Prayer we become alert to the grace and demands of the Kingdom of God. Our life is then shaped by the values of the Kingdom of God, like love and compassion, freedom and justice, concern for the poor and for the environment. We grow in wisdom to discern the presence of the Kingdom of God in the events of our life, in our motivations and activities. This gives us strength and inner light to live according to the values of the Gospel. It means a transfer from the ego-sense to a conscious oneness with the Divine. In the *Way of the Pilgrim*, who practiced Jesus Prayer intensely, we read: "Sometimes my heart would feel as if it were bursting with joy, so light was it and full of freedom and consolation.

Sometimes I would feel a burning love towards Jesus Christ and all of God's creatures...Sometimes, by invoking the name of Jesus, I was overcome with happiness, and from then on I knew the meaning of these words: the kingdom of God is within you".[1] As we move out of the centre of our being, God moves in. Through the practice of the prayer of the name of Jesus we become increasingly liberated from ego-centredness and grow into the process of the Kingdom of God. Theophan the Recluse says: "The man dwells inwardly before God without ceasing; this is the establishing of the Kingdom of God within us. With this comes the beginning of a new cycle of changes in inner life: the spiritualization of soul and body."[2]

5.   A Deep Trust in God

Jesus Prayer deepens the conviction that our life unfolds within the Divine. We feel that we are safe in the hands of God at every moment. We have a strong faith that nothing happens in our life unless permitted by God. By invoking the name of Jesus we experience Christ as the foundation stone, source of strength and inner fountain of our life. Life unfolds from Christ within. This gives a tremendous trust, joy in life and freedom from fear. The *Catechism of the Catholic Church* states: "The invocation of the holy name of Jesus is the simplest way of praying always. This prayer is possible at all times, because it is not one occupation among others, but the only occupation, that of loving God, which animates and transfigures every action in Christ Jesus" (§2668).

6.   Living in the Present

While practising Jesus Prayer we are consciously present to the present moment. Our mind is fully focused on the divine name without getting distracted. Thus we develop the ability to be more attentive to the present moment. Waking to the divine depth of the present moment is a grace; this is eternity. Eternity is the divine depth dimension of the present moment (*nunc aeternum*). Living in the present means that we are able to see the hand of God in the events of our daily life, in whatever happens. This is the experience of living in the Kingdom of God. Repetition of the name of Jesus leads us to the depth dimension of life. This adds a new quality to our life.

7.   Freedom from Loneliness

In today's world many people experience a deep-rooted loneliness. In spite of interpersonal relationships in marriage and friendship, there is a painful feeling that deep within we are lonely. This existential loneliness cannot be overcome by social contacts alone. We need to experience the inner divine well-springs. Jesus Prayer gives us an abiding sense of the indwelling presence of Christ in us. This is participation in the consciousness of Christ: "I am not alone, the Father is with me" (Jn. 8:16, 28-29; 16:32). Through the invocation of the name of Jesus we grow into the awareness that we are not alone, but we are always guided by the Spirit of Christ, we are loved by the divine Father. With this we can accept ourselves and face life with joy and confidence.

8.   Awakening to the Presence of Christ in the Universe

As described in the Logos-hymn of John's Gospel, everything has been created through the Word; the Word is the *life* of all beings and the *light* of humans. Through the repetition of the divine name we wake to the awareness of this cosmic presence of the divine Word. In the Chandogya Upanishad, it is said that everything has been created through the vibration of the divine sound OM (Chand. Up. 1.5.1). Through meditation we listen to the vibration of OM. When through Jesus Prayer we wake to the presence of Christ in the cave of the heart, we realise that the same presence of Christ is shining through all beings in creation. Creatures are then seen as manifestation of the Creator (*Theophany*). This is the experience of the presence of Christ filling the entire universe (*Christophany*). Through Jesus Prayer we open ourselves to the process of the divine Spirit renewing the face of the earth. In the presence of the indwelling Christ we look at humans and things of nature in a new way. In the song of the birds, in the music of the wind, in the dance of flowers, in the dazzling light of the sun, in the refreshing rain fall...in everything we feel the presence of God. In the *Way of the Pilgrim* it is said: "When I began to pray with the heart, everything around me became transformed and I saw it in a new and delightful way. The trees, the grass, the earth, the air, the light, and everything seemed to be saying to me that it exists to witness to God´s love for humans and that it prays and sings of God´s glory."[3] Thus the whole universe becomes the sacrament of God´s presence.

9.　　Respect for Other religions

Jesus Prayer awakens us to the divine presence here and now, in us and all around us. As Christians we have access to this mystical experience through Christ. Jesus Christ is the divine name for us to experience the divine presence. The Spirit of God works in the hearts of others in diverse ways. Hence the followers of other religions come to God-realisation through their own symbols and names of the Divine. The practice of Jesus Prayer opens our mind to the diverse ways of the divine Spirit in other religions. Hence we grow to respect and acknowledge the authentic experiences of God in the lives of believers of other religions. "We should have a deep respect for everything that has been brought about in human beings by the *Spirit who blows, where it wills.*" (John Paul II, *Redemptoris Missio, 56*)

10.　　Inner Purification

When we call on the name of Jesus with a humble and contrite heart, a purification takes place in us. This is the way of liberation. As a magnet brings iron particles into a definite order, Jesus Prayer harmonises the diverse elements of the mind and psyche, and purifies them. We are liberated from distractions and negative feelings. As a man walks with a torch in the darkness we walk through the dark realms of the subconscious psyche with the light of the practice of Jesus Prayer; the name of Jesus enables us to understand ourselves deeper and to get rid of the negative elements. While invoking the name of Jesus some elements of the subconscious psyche may surface at the conscious level of the mind, and these get purified in the light of the presence of Christ.

11. Control of the Mind

Our mind tends to get distracted with too many things and we become very restless and tired. Jesus Prayer makes the wandering mind anchored within the divine presence. Mind gets attuned to the divine movements within. Distracting thoughts and disturbing feelings are brought under control. One experiences genuine happiness and peace within. Through the practice of Jesus Prayer a profound peace of mind is sustained in the bustle of daily life. Heart gets filled with divine love. The sweetness of the name of Jesus becomes an intense experience.

12. Integral Healing

Jesus Prayer calms the mind and overcomes greed, integrates the psychic forces and harmonises the emotions, deepens the awareness of the present moment and anchors the human self in the divine Self. This promotes the general health and well-being of humans. In moments of sickness and helplessness, Jesus Prayer can be a healing experience. There is a difference between overcoming sickness and experiencing integral healing; the first is related to the physical body, the latter is a holistic process. In moments of sickness and pain one may experience through the practice of Jesus Prayer the divine healing energies flowing out of the inner well-springs. Those who are elderly and bedridden, unable to make long prayers, could find in Jesus Prayer a simple but powerful way of praying to attain inner peace and trust in God. This form may even render them with a tangible healing experience of the divine presence.

13.   Seeing Christ in the Suffering Humans

Through Jesus Prayer we are sensitivised to perceive Christ in the poor and the sick, in the suffering and marginalised people. We are graced with the ability to read the hearts of others (*kardiognosis*). "The name of Jesus frees people from mental distraction, puts devils to flight, cures the sick, infuses a wonderful meekness and tranquillity of character, love for humanity and kindness and gentleness" (Origen, *Contra Celsum, 1, 67*).[4] We become more compassionate. We understand deeper the meaning of the words of Jesus: I was hungry, I was thirsty, I was sick....Compassion is the fruit of contemplation.

14.   A Deeper Insight into the Holy Scripture

Through the practice of the Jesus Prayer the faculty of insight (*nous/ buddhi*) is attuned to the divine wisdom. With this we are enabled to re-read and interpret the Holy Scripture with an intuitive eye enlightened by the Spirit. Thus we discover the deeper meaning of the Word of God vibrating in the words of the Scripture.

15.   Jesus Prayer Refreshes our Soul

As sunlight passes through a tree, the tree gets life-giving warmth and light; similarly the light of Christ passes through our life intensely when we practise Jesus Prayer. The divine presence filling the universe flashes into our mind and heart. We are filled with the divine vibrations. And thus we are attuned to divine presence everywhere. Like a lens Jesus prayer condenses the divine energies and passes them to the soul. Jesus Prayer is the prism of the divine Spirit, prism of the divine presence in the cosmos, sacrament of the divine presence in the universe.

The *Pilgrim* describes the fruits of Jesus Prayer as he experienced them: "The fruits of Jesus Prayer can be experienced in three ways:

in the spirit, in the emotions, and in revelations. In the spirit one can experience the sweetness of the love of God, inner peace, purity of thought, awareness of God's presence and ecstasy. In the emotions one experiences a pleasant warmth of the heart, a feeling of delight throughout one's being, joyful bubbling in the heart, lightness and courage, joy of life and indifference to sickness and sorrow. And in revelation one receives the enlightenment of the mind, understanding of Holy Scripture, knowledge of speech of all creatures, renunciation of vanities, awareness of the sweetness of interior life, and confidence in the nearness of God and his love for us."[5]

Endnotes

[1] cit. Gillet (1987) p. 82.

[2] cit. Chariton (1996), p. 169.

[3] *Way of the Pilgrim* (1978), p. 34.

[4] cit. Gillet (1987),p. 29.

[5] *Way of the Pilgrim* (1978), p. 41.

IV

12
Different Ways of Practising Jesus Prayer

For the practice of Jesus Prayer different ways are recommended by spiritual masters. These are helps to make us more receptive to the movements of the Spirit. Union of the soul with God is ultimately a gift of grace.

Invocation of the Name of Jesus

For invocation of the name of Jesus the spiritual masters teach that the formula should be short and resonating with one´s heart; once a formula is chosen, it should not be changed too frequently: like plants that are often transplanted do not take root. For the practice: become aware of the presence of God. Implore the help of the Holy Spirit. With loving adoration and self-surrender repeat the name of Jesus. Focus the entire attention on the name and feel its inner spiritual power. Concentrate on the indwelling presence of the Risen Christ in the heart. Mechanical repetition is not the effective way. Let the Spirit impregnate the soul. Surrender all thoughts and images to the inner movement of the Spirit. After repeating the name for some time one could have moments of repose for a meditative assimilation of the power of the name. This is something like a bird in the air alternating between the flapping of its wings and gliding in the air.

Chanting the Name of Jesus

In Jesus Prayer rhythmic chanting leads the mind to stillness and silence. One uses a very simple melody, so that the attention is focused not on the melody of the chanting but on the inner presence of Christ. Gradually the mind becomes still and serene; spontaneously the chanting ceases and one calls on the name in deep silence within the heart.

Writing the Name of Jesus

Writing the name of the Lord is a popular way of praying the name found in different religions. There are moments when one is disturbed and is not in a position to make formal prayer. In such moments one takes to writing the name of the Lord. One sits comfortably, concentrates on Christ within and with all the love and devotion writes the name of the Lord in a special book kept for it. While repeating a whole formula, one writes only name *Jesus*. Devotees keep a special book for this exercise. This book filled with the name of the Lord is considered to be a spiritual treasure. Writing the name can be done anywhere and anytime.

Repeating the Name of Jesus along with the Breath

Many spiritual masters recommend the repetition of the name of the Lord with the breath. "Let the memory of Jesus combine with your breath" (John Klimakus, *Ladder, 27. PG. 88. 1112C*).[1] When we concentrate on the breath the mind becomes calm and still. Take a few moments and concentrate on the in-breath and out-breath. Place the name of *Jesus* on the incoming breath and repeat *mercy* or any other word with the outgoing breath. Continue this for some time. As the pranah energy penetrates the body, become aware of the divine name permeating the whole body. Feel the negativity vanishing through the out-breath. St. Nikephoros (14th cent) teaches: "Breathing is a natural way to the heart. In order to bring the mind to the heart, concentrate on the breath and repeat the name of Jesus."[2]

Repeating the Name of Jesus along with the Heart-beat

At the beginning it may be difficult to feel the heart-beat. One could feel the pulse-rate which is the same as the heart-beat. Feel the pulse at the wrist and repeat the name *Jesus* along with it. Once you get attuned to the rhythm of the pulse-rate, go on repeating the name with that rhythm for some time. Then there is no need to feel the pulse anymore. As you continue to repeat the name with the rhythm of the pulse, try to sense the slight vibration in the heart-centre; repeat the name along with the vibration. Gradually one is enabled to recognise the heart-beat with the vibration; then repeat the name of Jesus with every heart-beat. After some time bring attention to the indwelling presence of Christ in the *heart* along with the repetition. This can be a beautiful experience of praying the name of Jesus. One feels that the repetition comes to a stop spontaneously: I do not repeat the name, it repeats. I listen to the name of Jesus being repeated from within. It is an experience of the name of Jesus taking root in the *heart*. As Paul explains, the Spirit prays from within our heart (Rom. 8:26). "No one can say, Jesus is the Lord, except in the Holy Spirit" (I Cor. 12:3). In the *Way of a Pilgrim* we read:

"I closed my eyes and imagined looking into my heart; my desire was to visualise the heart in the left breast and to listen attentively to its beating. At the beginning I was not aware of anything but darkness; slowly the heart appeared and I noticed its movement. While looking into the heart and inhaling I said, *Lord Jesus Christ*, and while exhaling *have mercy on me*...Sometimes I experienced a sweet burning in my heart, at other times a burning love for Jesus Christ and all of God's creation."[3]

Jesus Prayer in Walking

Pronounce the name of Jesus with every step. As the heel touches the ground say *Je-* and as the toes slowly touch the ground say *–sus*, recognising the indwelling Christ as the Ground of being, the source and foundation of life. Throughout the walking Christ is realised as the indwelling Christ. In him and with him and through him every step is taken. Christ is the subject within: he walks with us, through us, in us. "Jesus is the one who walks always beside us when we are at the extremity of our strength, who is with us in the wilderness of ice or in the furnace of fire. To each of us, at the time of our greatest loneliness or trial, this word is said: you are not alone, you have a companion" (Kallistos Ware).[4] We participate in the experience of Jesus as he experienced the Father within him. Thus one experiences Christ as the constant companion. The steps we take in walking meditation can represent our entire life-journey.

Jesus Prayer with Body Posture

In the Middle Ages body was very much associated with the practice of Jesus Prayer through postures like kneeling, bowing, prostration, extending the hands in the form of a Cross. Jesus Prayer thus gets a holistic significance integrating the body with the soul. "Sit down or – better still – stand in a prayerful position; concentrate the attention in the heart. If you wish accompany this with bows from the waste or else with prostrations" (Theophan the Recluse).[5] What follows is a simple method with body postures: We use the formula: "*Śree Yesu Christāya namō namah.*" Hold the palms folded (*anjali*) above the head and chant *Śree Yesu Christāya*, recognizing Christ as the Lord of the universe. Then bring the palms in *anjali* posture to the heart-centre and chant *namō,* recognizing Christ abiding within the heart. Then open the palms as an open vessel chanting *namah* and surrender oneself to the divine Lord.

Jesus Prayer in Nature

The whole creation evolves from the divine Logos: "Through him all things came into being" (Jn. 1:2). "Every visible or invisible creature is a theophany or appearance of God" (John Scotus).[6]

Creation becomes a sacrament of God´s presence. "Wherever you turn your eyes there is God´s symbol; wherever you read you will find there his types" (Ephrem the Syrian).[7] The Logos became flesh in Jesus Christ (Jn. 1:14). "Everything is created in him, through him and unto him" (Col. 1:15-18). This is an invitation to recognise the presence of Christ shining forth in the entire creation: in the beauty of nature, in the songs of the birds, in the fragrance of the flowers; this is Christophany. Nature is a sacred ambience. On this basis Jesus Prayer could be practiced in nature.

Pronounce the name of Jesus over every creature that one looks at; may the blessings of the divine name descent on that. Yahweh asks Moses to bless the Israelites by pronouncing the *name of God* on them (Num. 6:27). Nature and Scripture complement each other. It is said that the early Christians attributed to Christ this saying: "Lift the stone and you will find me; cut the wood in two and there am I".[8] One invokes the name of Jesus on the men and women whom one meets, recognising and silently adoring Christ in that person. The name can be pronounced upon the elements of nature, stars, trees, flowers, fruits, mountains, seas and so bring to fulfillment the groaning of creation towards Christ (Rom. 8:22) "All things are permeated and maintained in being by the uncreated energies of God, and so all things are a theophany that mediates his presence. At the heart of each thing is its inner principle (Logos), implanted within it by the Creator-Logos; and so through the logoi we enter into communion with the Logos. God is above and beyond all things, yet as Creator he is also within all things" (Kallistos Ware).[9]

Endnotes

[1] cit. *Writings from the Philokalia* (1995), p.85.

[2] cit. *Writings from the Philokalia* (1995), p. 33.

[3] *Way of a Pilgrim (1978)* p. 40-41.

[4] Ware, (1979), p. 89.

[5] cit. Chariton (1996), p. 114.

[6] cit. Ware (1979), p. 29.

[7] cit. Ware (1979), p. 162.

[8] cit. Ware (1979), p. 29.

[9] Ware (1979), p. 158.

13
Meditations with Jesus Prayer

Fifteen meditations with Jesus Prayer are offered here. Meditations 1-3 are helps to come to an inner silence; 4-13 propose some ways to practise Jesus Prayer within this silence; 14-15 are related to the fruits of the practise of Jesus Prayer. For each meditation (i) an inspiring story is given, (ii) a short reflection is offered, (iii) appropriate sayings of the spiritual masters are given, (iv) the method of meditation is proposed. In these meditations the following mantra forms are suggested. But each one has the freedom to choose a formula with which one can resonate; one can either repeat it or chant it with a melody. What is important is that the name *Jesus* must be in it.

Med. 4. *Sadguru Jesu… Sadguru Jesu… Sadguru Jesu… Sadguru Jesu…* (Jesus, the divine master)

Med. 5. *Jesu OM Jesu…*

Med. 6. *Om namō Christāya*   (I adore Christ)

Med. 7. *Jesu..Jesu..Jai Jai… Jesu…, Jesu…Jesu… namō …Jesu…* (Praise and adoration to Jesus)

Med. 8. *Jesu…Jesu… namō …namah…*   (Adoration to Jesus)

Med. 10. *Jesu…Jesu…Jesu…Christa…*

Med. 12. *Yesu-nāmam Jai…Jai…Christu- nāmam Jai…Jai…* (Praise to the name of Jesus, Praise to the name of Christ)

Med. 13. *Jesu Jīvan Jyōti…*   (Jesus, Light of life)

Med. 14. *Jesu..Jesu..Jesu Nām, Jesu…Jesu…Jesu Nām…* (name of Jesus)

Med. 15. *Śree Yesu…Jai Yesu..Jai Jai Yesu OM…* (Divine Jesus, praise to Jesus)

(A CD with the chanting of these mantras by Sr. Rose Pudukadan and team may be purchased with this book. It is also available at Sameeksha, Kalady, Kerala: ph. (0091)0484-2462805)

1. Sit Earthed

An old man was sitting on the roadside and begging. His family lived very poor with whatever he got. One day a monk came that way. Hoping to get some alms the beggar extended his hands. The monk said: I have no money to give you. On what are you sitting, asked the monk. The beggar replied: For many years I am sitting on this box that I found lying under this tree. Have you ever opened it? - asked the monk. No, he replied. The monk said: Open and see what is inside. The old man opened the box and to his surprise, he found the wooden box filled with diamonds and gold coins. The beggar realised that he was leading a miserable life, though all the while he was sitting on this treasure.

The spiritual masters say that we live like this old man not realising the divine treasure within us. We live very much depending on our capabilities and perceptions. Jesus Prayer is a way to discover the inner divine treasure in the *heart*. When we invoke the name of Jesus, we open our mind and heart to the indwelling presence of Christ. His grace flows into us, his Spirit enriches our life.

"The Kingdom of heaven is like treasure hidden in a field" (Mt. 13:44).

"Enter eagerly into the treasure-house that is within you and so you will see the treasure-house of heaven; the ladder that leads to the Kingdom of God is hidden within your soul" – Isaac the Syrian.[1]

"The Kingdom of God is the innermost realm of the ground of being, in the hiddenness of the Spirit that resonates with the divine abyss" – Johannes Tauler, *Sermon 62.*

"Once the mind is united with the heart, one discovers the treasure hidden in the field, the pearl beyond price" – Theophan the Recluse.[2]

"Nature cannot be regarded as something separate from ourselves or as a mere setting in which we live. We are part of nature, included in it and thus in constant interaction with it" – Pope Francis, *Laudato si, §139.*

Meditation

I sit straight and relaxed, preferably on the floor, close to the earth. Slowly I feel into the earth. All my attention is brought downward. As a baby sitting on the lap of the mother I sit on the earth and sense the life-bearing energies of the mother earth. I become aware of the oneness between my body and the earth. I also feel myself closely united with all that grows out of the earth: humans, animals and birds, plants and trees. I listen to the chirping of the birds, the music of the raindrops, the sound of the breeze. I sit in harmony with lakes and rivers, hills and plains. I try to resonate with the silence of the mother earth.

The entire attention is brought inward, to the indwelling divine presence, the treasure within me.

2.   Feel the Body

There is a sufi story. God spoke to the prophet: "Between you and me there are 70000 veils. These hide my face from you. But between me and you there are no veils; I see you clearly at every moment". These veils which hide the indwelling presence of God from our perception are our undue attachments to the things of this world, desire for name and fame, for prestige and fortune. Jesus Prayer enables us to overcome this ego-centredness.

The sun may be shining bright outside, but if the windows and doors of my room are closed I stay in darkness. Only if I open the windows and doors can I experience the sunlight that beams into the room. Though the divine sun is ever shining in our heart, only when we open our mind and heart to the divine presence do we relish it. Jesus Prayer is a means by which we open ourselves to the Divine within.

There may be several light systems in a room. Only when we put on the switch the electricity flows and we experience the light. Jesus Prayer is a means to open ourselves to the energy-stream of the divine Spirit.

The diamond shines bright; if it is covered with dirt and dung one cannot experience the natural brightness of the diamond. When the diamond is cleaned, it begins to shine. As long as our mind is filled with worries and anxieties we cannot sense the enlightening divine presence. Jesus Prayer brings about inner enlightenment by which the divine presence can be experienced within.

"No one lights a lamp and puts it in some hidden place or under a bushel, but on a lamp-stand, so that those who enter may see the light" (Lk. 11:33).

"In the case of the first Adam, earth was changed into flesh; in the case of the second Adam, flesh was raised up to be God" - Peter Chrysologus, *Sermon, 117.*

"Being God the Logos assumed the flesh, and being in the flesh, he deified the flesh" - Athanasius, *Contra Arian. 3.38.*

"The body is deified along with the soul through its own corresponding participation in the process of deification" - Maximus the Confessor, *Capita Theologica, 2.88. PG. 91. 1168a.*[3]

"Being the sun of our intellect the name of Jesus creates within it luminous thoughts to which it communicates its own splendour, resembling the sun" - Hesychius, *The Centuries, PG. 93. 1480.*[4]

Meditation

I sit straight and relaxed, preferably on the floor, close to the earth. I bring attention to the body. First I become aware of the vital centre: I feel through the entire abdomen with love and gratitude. Then I move slowly towards the feet, then return to the vital centre and move upward towards the hands; finally I return to the vital centre. I do this awareness exercise with love and respect for the body, as an inner pilgrimage through the *temple of the Spirit* that I am. During the entire meditation I stay with the awareness that my body is a sacred space.

I sense the bodily silence that evolves. In this bodily silence I wake to the divine presence that permeates my body.

3.   Feel the Breath

Usually a goldsmith makes fire in a fire-pan. In that fire he melts gold to make ornaments. Every night before he goes home he sprinkles water over it to put off the fire. In the morning when he begins his work, he cleans the fire-pan and removes the ashes. Deep in the fire-pan he always finds a spark of fire; he places coconut-charcoal over it and blows into the spark. Slowly the spark gives rise to a flame. He keeps on blowing into the furnace until it comes to blazing. Through his breath the spark evolves into fire.

There is a divine spark deep within our heart. Jesus Prayer is a means for fanning it to fire. Through the repetition of the name of Jesus the divine presence within us unfolds through the power of the Spirit (divine breath). With this awakening one is enabled to shape life according to the movements of the Spirit.

"God gives everything life and breath" (Acts 17:25)

"May the remembrance of Jesus be united to your breathing and to your whole life" - Hesychius, *The Centuries, I.99.*

"May the remembrance of Jesus be united to your breathing and then you will know the value of hesychia" - John Klimakus, *Ladder, 27, 61. PG. 88. 1112C.*[5]

"Breathing is the natural way to the heart. In order to bring the mind to the heart, concentrate on the breath, and repeat the name of Jesus" - Nikephoros[6]

"Looking at one's breath can be as fascinating as looking at a river. It can still the mind, and so give rise to wisdom, silence and a sense of the Divine. You breathe not only through your nostrils but also through every pore" - Tony de Mello. [7]

Meditation

Sitting straight and relaxed I bring attention to breathing. While breathing *in* I gratefully let the energy of life flow into the body. While breathing *out* I feel the *prāna* energy percolating through the legs and the hands: through the whole body. Gradually I feel all the cells of my body watered by the stream of *prāna*. In every breath I realise: *the breath of God breathes through me* (Job, 33:4; Acts, 17:25). Concentration on the breath is a simple but effective means to silence the mind and bring it to stillness.

The spark of the divine presence in my heart evolves into a flame through the divine breath.

4.   Devotional Surrender

Jesus came to the disciples walking on the water (Mt. 14:22-33). Peter asked Jesus whether he could come to him on the waters. Jesus said to him, come. Looking into the compassionate eyes of Jesus, Peter walked on the waters towards the master. He was totally unaware of the sea and storm and waves. His whole attention was focused on the divine Lord. Even the powers of nature and laws of nature were not able to touch him; he went beyond them. After a while Peter turned his attention away from the master and looked at the sea and felt the storm. Suddenly he began to sink.

When we focus attention on the divine Lord we can master the obstacles of life. The moment we rely too much on ourselves and turn away from God, we get lost. Jesus Prayer is a means to fix attention on the divine master and steer through the struggles of life.

"Whatever you ask in my name you will receive so that your joy may be full" (Jn. 16:24)

"The name of Jesus is nectar in the mouth, honey on the tongue, a serene light in the eyes, sound of life in the ears. It is living ambrosia. If you have tasted it but once, you cannot endure to be parted from it" - Paulinus of Nola, *PL. 61. 741A.*[8]

"Jesus Prayer must be breathed continually. The name of Jesus comes into our life first of all as a lamp in the darkness, next it is like moonlight and finally like the sun rise. Being the sun of our intellect it creates within it luminous thoughts to which it communicates its own splendour, resembling the sun" - Hesychius *The Centuries, PG. 93. 1480-1544.*[9]

"The more Jesus Prayer penetrates into the heart, the warmer the heart becomes, and the more self-impelled becomes the prayer, so that the fire of spiritual life is kindled in the heart and its burning becomes unceasing" - Theophan the Recluse.[10]

Meditation

I sit relaxed. Keeping the palms as an open vessel in front of the heart I surrender myself totally to Jesus the divine master. Focusing the attention on the inner presence of Christ I chant the name of Jesus with a formula like *Sadguru Jesu… Sadguru Jesu… Sadguru Jesu… Sadguru Jesu…*Jesus Prayer begins with an intense I-thou relationship with the Lord.

This devotional self-surrender gives an inner strength to steer through the struggles of life.

5.   Called to a Higher Consciousness

A sufi story: A duck's egg was put under a hen for hatching. When the egg hatched, the duckling walked about with the chicks under the protection of the mother hen. Once they came to a pond; the duckling walked straight into the water. Clucking anxiously the mother hen stayed on the bank. The sufi said: I have walked into the divine ocean and found in it my home.

A farmer was walking through the jungle. He found a new born little bird on the path. He took it affectionately in the hand and brought it home. Eating the worms and insects this little bird grew up with the chicks under the protection of the hen. One day a man came and found that this little bird does not belong to the family of the chicks. He took it in the hand and helped it to fly up; but the little one preferred to move with the chick companions. Another day he took it to a hill-top and kept it facing the sun. Fly, you little one; the sky, not the earth is your home, he said. Suddenly it took courage, spread the wings and soared high: it was an eaglet.

When one discovers one's divine identity, one soars high to the freedom of the skies. In every human person there is a relentless quest for the Divine; true freedom comes only when one realises the fulfillment of this quest in the Divine.

Jesus Prayer liberates us from being bonded to the world and its allurements.

"All who believe in the name of Jesus are given the grace to become the children of God" Jn. 1:12.

"The glory of God is the living man, *Gloria Dei homo vivens*" - Irenaeus, *Adv. Haer. 4.20.7*.

"Remain in the devout repetition of the name of Jesus Christ, so that the heart absorbs the divine Lord and the Lord captures the heart; both become one" - John Chrysostom, *PG. 60, 75*.

"Through the remembrance of Jesus the heart is purified and inflamed" - Diadochus, Bishop of Photike, *Hundred Chapters on Perfection, 97*.[11]

"I was overwhelmed with the desire to recite the Jesus Prayer. And when I started it, it became so easy and delightful that my tongue and lip seemed to do it of themselves. I was joyful the whole day" - *Way of the Pilgrim*.[12]

Meditation

I come to a deep inner silence. In interior silence I chant *Jesu OM Jesu*... The vibration of the divine name of Jesus and the mantra OM lead me to a deeper contemplative silence. Within the heart I feel the indwelling presence of Christ. In that experience I recognise that I am called to a higher consciousness: I am a daughter / son of God.

Chanting of the Jesus-mantra raises / deepens our consciousness unto the realisation: *I am divine.*

6.   The Master's Touch

There was an old violin in an auctioneer's shop. Every day the auctioneer will bring it out to be auctioned off. Nobody wanted to buy it, because it was too old and the strings were loose. One day a grey haired man from the crowd came forward, picked up the violin, polished it, tightened and tuned the strings and started to play the violin. He played a melody pure and sweet. People were amazed to hear such a melody coming out of that old violin. When he finished playing he handed it over to the auctioneer. It was sold out for a high price. Someone asked: how this miraculous change? Swift came the reply: the touch of the master's hand.

Very often we are like this old violin. When we place ourselves in the hands of the divine master, he can bring forth great melodies from within us. For this we have to let go our hold on the ego-self and realise our true-self which is *Christ within the heart*.

"In the name of Jesus Christ get up and walk" (Acts 3:6)

"Let your prayer be completely simple. Let there be no studied elegance in the words of your prayers. Prolixity in prayer often fills the mind with images and distracts it, whereas the use of one single word (*monologia*) draws it into recollection. The beginning of prayer consists in banishing the thoughts that come to us by the use of a single word the very moment they appear (*monologistos*)" - John Climacus, *The Ladder, 28*

"Whoever says too much in prayer, does not pray, but indulges in idle talk" - John Chrysostom, *Commentary on St. Paul.* [13]

"You should not make long prayers, for it is better to pray little but often. Superfluous words are idle talk" - St. Theophylact, *Commentary on the Gospel of Mathew, 6,7.*[14]

"In order not to fall into illusion while praying the name of Jesus do not permit any visual concept, image or vision in the mind" - Nil Sorsky.[15]

Meditation

I become aware of myself. I take note of the areas where I am out of tune: the tensions, worries, anxieties and sinfulness. Fully accepting myself as I have become, I surrender myself to the hands of the divine master by chanting *OM namō Christāyā*...His divine touch brings healing into my life. I become a new creation through the master´s touch. With a new self-esteem I emerge as a free and joyful person.

Jesus Prayer leads to a deep contemplative silence beyond words and tunes us to the melody of the divine Spirit.

7.   Inner Purification

A guru had two disciples. One of the disciples felt that the master likes the other one more than him. His mind was very much disturbed by anger and envy. He told the master, I feel, you love the other disciple more than you love me. The master gave 10 Rs to both the disciples. He told them to go to the market and buy all that they can get with this amount and fill their room with it; and he will come in the evening to check it. The complaining disciple did not succeed in getting anything for Rs. 10 to fill the room. Then he saw a truck coming with stinking garbage. The disciple gave the 10 Rs. to the driver and told him to dump the whole thing in his room. In the evening the master came and saw the room filled with stinking garbage. He went to the other disciple´s room. A small candle was lit and two incense sticks were burning. The candle light and the incense sticks filled the room with light and sweet fragrance. The master called the disciples and told them: Never allow a negative thought or feeling fill your mind. When the mind is filled with negativity, the divine inspiration cannot enter there. The divine inspiration can be received only in an empty mind and pure heart.

When we allow negative thoughts enter our mind we cannot recognise the divine presence from within. Negative feelings block the mind from receiving the divine fragrance in the heart.

"In my name you will cast out the powers of evil; in my name you will lay your hands on the sick, and they will recover" (Mk. 16:17)

"The name of Jesus frees people from mental distraction, puts devils to flight, cures the sick, infuses a wonderful meekness and tranquillity of character, love for humanity and kindness and gentleness" - Origen, *Contra Celsum, 1, 67.*[16]

"It is enough to invoke the name of Christ to put evil forces to flight" - Athanasius, PG. 25.181B

"The head is a crowded rag market: it is not possible to pray to God there" – Theophan the Recluse.[17]

"The name of Jesus was contained in Israel like perfume in a closed vessel. Now the vessel has been opened and the perfume has spread everywhere. There has been a real outpouring of this name, and outpouring or overflowing of grace" - Ambrose, *De Spiritu Sancto*, I. VIII. 96, PL. 16. 727D.[18]

Meditation

In all sincerity I become aware of the garbage in my mind: the negative elements stinking in me. I accept myself as I have become and surrender me to the divine master by chanting *Jesu..Jesu..Jai Jai… Jesu…, Jesu…Jesu… namō…Jesu…* Jesus Prayer evokes spiritual vibrations in me and fills the heart with a divine fragrance. The power of the negativities is overcome by the positive stream of the divine Light.

8.   Trust in the Power of the Name

An ashramite relates the following experience he had. He was living all alone in a forest hut intensely practicing Jesus Prayer. One day at noon he was walking beside a stream. Suddenly he heard a loud sound. Turning back he saw a wild elephant running towards him. Terrified by that sight he ran to his hut, took the cymbals and started chanting the name of Jesus in a loud voice. The elephant approached the hut and stood in front of it. With deep trust in the power of the name he went on chanting the name louder. The elephant began to swing to the tune of the chanting. This lasted for several minutes. He opened the eyes and found the elephant gently receding. A few days after this first encounter the same elephant ran after him again, but stayed by the hut enjoying the chanting.

Chanting the name of Jesus evokes powerful vibrations around us. Even the animals and the elements of nature can feel them. Even violent animals become gentle through these vibrations. The power of the name of Jesus brings us into harmony with the surroundings.

"...so that all beings should bend the knee at the name of name of Jesus and that every tongue should acclaim Jesus Christ as Lord" (Phil, 2:10-11)

"I know that he who is far outside the whole creation takes me within himself and hides me in his arms, and then I find myself outside the whole world; all of him is within myself. I have the divine life springing up as a fountain within me; he is in my heart" (Symeon the New Theologian.[19]

"When I began to pray with the heart, everything around me became transformed and I saw it in a new and delightful way. The trees, the grass, the earth, the air, the light, and everything seemed to be saying to me that it exists to witness to God's love for humans and that it prays and sings of God's glory - *Way of the Pilgrim*.[20]

"Jesus prayer awakens the presence of Christ in nature. This universe murmurs secretly the name of Jesus. It belongs to the priestly ministry of each Christian to give a voice to this aspiration, to pronounce the name of Jesus upon the elements of nature, stones and trees, flowers and fruits, mountains and sea, and so to bring to fulfilment to the secret of things, to provide and answer to that long silent and unconscious expectation" - Archimandrite Lev Gillet.[21]

Meditation

I go out into nature for meditation. I sit in a serene spot or I walk through the woods. I chant aloud the name of Jesus with a mantra like *Jesu…Jesu.. namō …namah…* I feel the power of the name that evolves in my heart. I sense the spiritual vibrations of the divine name percolating all around me: in the trees, rivers, hills, animals, birds… I become aware of the sacredness of the divine ambience around me. I wake to the experience of creation as Christophany.

9.   Resonance of the Name in the Heart

A genuine seeker was exploring the enlightening power of silence for several years in an ashram. He came to no enlightenment. One day he approached the master and asked, what more can I do to achieve enlightenment? So very little, the master answered, just as you cannot make the sun rise tomorrow. That disappointed the disciple. Why then should I pursue this hard discipline of life and the daily exercise of silence, he asked. The master answered: ...so that you do not sleep when the sun rises.

The experience of hesychia we cannot attain by our own effort; it is a gift of divine grace. All that we can do is to open our mind and heart to the power of the name of Jesus. The receptive attitude is important to experience the divine sun-rise in our life.

"Anything you ask for from the Father he will grant in my name" Jn. 16:23)

"We ought to give to the nous (intellect, *buddhi*) nothing but the words *Lord Jesus*" - Diadochos, Bishop of Photike, *Hundred Chapters on Perfection, 59.*[22]

"I closed my eyes and imagined looking into my heart; my desire was to visualise the heart in the left breast and to listen attentively to its beating. At the beginning I was not aware of anything but darkness; slowly the heart appeared and I noticed its movement. While looking into the heart and inhaling I said, *Lord Jesus Christ*, and while exhaling *have mercy on me*...Sometimes I experienced a sweet burning in my heart, at other times a burning love for Jesus Christ and all of God's creation" - *Way of a Pilgrim.*[23]

"We are to call to mind Jesus Christ until the name of the Lord penetrates our heart, descends to its very depths and gives life to the soul" - Nikephoros, *PG.147, 965-966.*

Meditation

I sit straight and relaxed in a serene place. I bring attention to the heart where Christ is the ever shining divine sun. To perceive the inner light of Christ I have to still the mind, get to the nous and enter the heart. For this I become aware of the heart-beat and invoke the name of Jesus along with it (p. 109). Once I get attuned to this rhythm, I draw attention to the indwelling presence of Christ in the spiritual *heart*. After some time the repetition stops spontaneously and I feel as if I listen to the name of Jesus being repeated from within. I sit in a receptive attitude in his presence.

10.   Merging with the Divine

A salt doll in the mountain heard of the sea. It wanted to see the sea. It made a long way walking up and down the mountain and finally it reached the sea-shore. Amazed by the vastness of the sea it asked: who are you? The sea replied: walk into me and then you will know who I am. The salt doll glided into the waters. Then it realised its true nature.

As long as God is looked upon as someone before or above us we do not really experience the divine presence within. Though the invocation of the name of Jesus begins as a vocal prayer, soon the repetition recedes into contemplative silence. I chant the name of the Lord with a mantra like, *Jesu.....Jesu....Jesu...*In the silence of the heart I realise my true nature. Only by merging into the Divine do I realise who the Divine is, and who I am truly.

"Father, keep them in thy name, which thou hast given me, that they may be one, even as we are one" (Jn. 17:11).

"The one who knows God, becomes God-like" - Thomas Aquinas, *quisque Deum intelligt, deiformis fit, ST. 1.12.5.ad.3.*

"The one who knows the Divine becomes divine" Mundaka Up, 3.2.9, *brahmavid brahmaiva bhavati.*

"Only by becoming ONE can you realise the Divine in you" - Meister Eckhart, *On the noble man.*

"The soul reaches a resemblance of God" - Cyril of Alexandria, PG. 10. 109 ab.

"The name of the Son of God is great and boundless, and it is this that upholds the entire world" - *Shepherd of Hermas*, III.9.14.[24]

Meditation

I sit surrendering myself to Christ the Lord. I experience him first as the divine thou, whom I long for. Praying the name of Jesus begins with this devotional self-surrender. Gradually my consciousness sinks to the heart, wherein I experience the indwelling presence of Christ. I chant the divine name with a mantra like *Jesu...Jesu...Jesu...Christa...*As the salt doll realises its true being by merging into the sea, I merge into the presence of Christ and discover the divinity within me. Only by becoming one with the Divine can I experience the Divine.

11.   Unceasing Awareness

In the master's household a maidservant looks after the children with love and tenderness: she feeds them, clothes them, bathes them and takes care of them. While she cares for the children of the master, she can never forget her own children at home. Deep in her heart there is always a loving concern and longing for her children, who are always present to her.

Even when we are engaged in different activities, there should be an inner awareness of the divine presence in the heart. There we are truly at home. It is the love that comes from the heart that gives us spiritual energy in our activities. Jesus Prayer is a simple but effective way to get in touch with this inner divine presence. A concrete way of practicing it is to get recollected in the midst of activities for a few seconds and become aware of the indwelling presence of Christ by invoking the name of Jesus.

"Whatever you say or do, do it in the name of Jesus giving thanks to the Father through him" Col. 3:17.

"Whether one eats or drinks, sits or serves, travels or does anything else, must unceasingly cry out Jesus Prayer. In this way the name of the Lord will descent into the depth of the heart, so that the heart may absorb the Lord and the Lord absorbs the heart, and the two become one. Do not severe your heart from God, but dwell with him until the name of the Lord is deeply rooted there and you cease to think of anything else" - John Chrysostom, *PG. 60, 75.*[25]

"The invocation of the holy name of Jesus is the simplest way of praying always. This prayer is possible at all times, because it is not one occupation among others, but the only occupation, that of loving God, which animates and transfigures every action in Christ Jesus" - *The Catechism of the Catholic Church, §2668*

Meditation

This meditation can be practiced in the midst of the activities of the day. Stay recollected for a few seconds and invoke the name of Jesus to get into communion with the indwelling presence of Christ. Bring awareness to breathing. With every in-breath say mentally *Jē-* and with the out-breath say interiorly *sū-* This could be repeated for a few times without in any way changing the rhythm of breathing. It is important to practise this in a very relaxed way with a certain spontaneity and self-surrender. This can be practised while cooking, gardening, travelling, driving, reading etc; this is especially helpful while lying in bed awaiting sleep.

12. Divine Revelation

Moses came to Horeb, the mountain of God. The divine presence appeared to him in a flame blazing from the middle of a bush. But the bush was not being burnt up. Moses went closer to the bush to see the strange thing. God called to him from the bush: take off you sandals, for the place where you are standing is holy ground (Ex. 3:1-6).

The bush was not burnt up, because it was filled with the presence of God. In our life when we face struggles, when we walk through fire, we are able to go through them if we are filled with the presence of God. It is not the bush that calls out Moses but God calling out from the bush and sending him forth on a mission. When we experience God within, he becomes the subject within us; we become instruments in God´s hands. Jesus Prayer helps us to be filled with the presence of God, experience the indwelling Christ and be moved by the Spirit.

"God has highly exalted him and bestowed on him the name which is above every name" (Phil. 2:9).

136

"By becoming as we are, the Logos makes us as he is" - Gregory of Nyssa, *Antirrheticus adv. Apollinarium, 11*

"He gave us divinity, we gave him humanity" - *Ephrem the Syrian, Hymni der Fide, 31, 5.7.*

"We do not choose the Prayer of Jesus, we are led to it by the Spirit. The Spirit writes the name of Jesus in fiery letters upon our hearts. The name is a burning flame within us" - Archimandrite Lev Gillet.[26]

"Unceasing prayer serves to maintain the inner fire, the burning of the Spirit"- John Chrysostom.[27]

"The name of Jesus appears first of all as a lamp in the darkness, next like the moonlight and finally like a sunrise" - Hesychius, *The Centuries, II.64.*[28]

Meditation

Spiritual masters look at Moses going up the Mount of Horeb as a symbol of the soul's ascent to the divine realms. I become aware of this spiritual ascent in me. I chant the name of Jesus with a mantra like: *Yesunāmam Jai… Jai…Christunāmam Jai…Jai.*.As I chant the divine name I sense the feeling of Moses going up the Mountain of God. Out of the incomprehensible mystery of the Divine I hear the name of Jesus as God-with-us, God-within-us (*Emmanuel*).Through Jesus Prayer I wake to the indwelling presence of Christ; I experience myself as an instrument in the divine mission.

13.   In Christ

The little fish was living happily in the ocean. One day it asked the mother fish: where is the ocean? Everyone speaks of the ocean; I want to see the ocean. The mother fish answered: little one, you are living and growing in the ocean, the ocean is within you and all around you; realise that. But the small fish was not satisfied with the answer. It went on asking every fish: where is the ocean?

Though at every moment we live and grow in the Divine, we do not recognise this truth. In fact our life evolves within the divine ocean. One looks for God as an object everywhere; but we do not realise that we are in the divine ocean. Jesus Prayer helps us to be awakened to this vibrant presence within and all around; it makes one experience that ´we live and move and have our being´ in Christ (Acts, 17:28).

"God gave him the name which is above all other names" Phil. 2:9.

"Let us become as Christ is, since Christ became as we are; let us become gods for his sake, since he became man for our sake" - Gregory of Nazianzen, *Orationes, 1.5.*

"We have not just become Christians; we have become Christ. Stand firm in awe and rejoice: we have become Christ! Christ speaks in us, prays in us, suffers in us, and lives in us. We are he! (*nos ipse sumus*) - Augustine, *PL. 35, 1568, 1929.*

"What man is, Christ was willing to be, so that man may also be what Christ is"- Cyprian, *Treatise VI, On the Vanity of Idols.*

God makes those who are found worthy of God reborn in grace to what Christ by nature is. He wants that we become what he is" - Symeon the New Theologian, *Hymn 44.*

Meditation

I sit in silence and get interiorly recollected. I try to sense the feeling of the fish in the ocean. Being immersed in the presence of Christ as in the divine ocean I chant the name with a Jesus mantra like *Jesu Jīvan Jyōti*... I feel the Christ-vibrations within my heart and all around. With the words invoked in the mantra I wake to the respective grace: peace (*śānthi*), salvation (*mukti*), power (*śakti*), breath (*prāna*), wisdom (*jnāna*), way (*mārga*)...

14. Prophetic Justice

The story of the encounter of David with Goliath (I Sam. 17.) gives a lot of insight into the power of the divine name. "David took with him only the sling and the five smooth stones... David said to Goliath: you come to me with sword, spear and scimitar; I come to you in the name of Yahweh. God will deliver you into my hands" (I Sam. 17:40-47). David put his complete trust in the name of Yahweh. Goliath trusting on the power of his weapons rushed to the young David to kill him. David gently took out a stone, slung it and struck Goliath on the forehead. The stone penetrated his skull and he fell face downwards on the ground. Thus David triumphed over the Philistines with the power of the name of Yahweh.

When we put complete trust in the power of the name of God in the journey of life, the name empowers us to advance with confidence. Praying the name of Jesus gives us an experience of this spiritual power. We face courageously social evils and all forms of injustice with the power of the divine name.

"Where two or three are gathered in my name, there I am in their midst" (Mt. 18:20)

"Thirst after Jesus and he will satisfy you with his love" - Isaac the Syrian.[29]

"Love makes human beings divine" – Maximus the Confessor, *Epistulae, 2. PG. 91. 393c; 401c*

"Every visible or invisible creature is a theophany or appearance of God" - John Scotus.[30]

"Wherever you turn your eyes there is God´s symbol; wherever you read you will find there his types" - Ephrem the Syrian.[31]

"Whoever takes on himself the burden of his neighbour, whoever supplies to the needy what he has received himself from God, becomes a *god* to those who receive from him; such a man is an imitator of God" - Tatian, *Epistle to Diognetus, 10.*

Meditation

I come to an inner silence. With full trust in the power of the name of the Lord I chant the divine name with a mantra like *Jesu..Jesu..Jesu Nām, Jesu... Jesu...Jesu Nām...* As I go on chanting I feel the spiritual power evolving in my heart and percolating into all my life situations. With that inner power I face the challenges of life; I recognise the presence of Christ in everyone I meet and in all events of life. This makes me sensitive to the demands of justice, the call for respect and change. I look at my life process as a movement in the divine Spirit that renews the face of the earth.

15. Mystical Compassion

A Christmas story: The schoolchildren were getting ready to put up a play on the scene of Mary and Joseph searching for a place to stay in Bethlehem. A little boy pleaded with the teacher to have a role in the drama. Though the teacher did not find him competent for this she yielded to his insistence. The boy got the role just to say *no room* to Mary and Joseph when they come. The performance got started. The boy saw Mary and Joseph, tired and worn out after a long journey, knocking at the inn. The boy said to them: "the teacher told me to tell you that there is no room for you here." Struggling with every step Mary and Joseph walked away. Moved to compassion the little boy ran after them and said:"Sorry, but there is a room in my home, please come."

As long as the boy had to play a role in the drama he had to abide by certain conditions. Outside of them he became true to himself; he became compassionate. In the drama of life we play a lot of forced roles; but deep down in our heart there is a spark of compassion which we have to fan to flame.

Jesus Prayer is a means to awaken compassionate attitudes in our life.

"Whoever receives a child in my name, receives me" (Mk. 9:37)

"Nothing brings us more easily either to justification or to divinisation, nothing is more apt to bring about closeness to God, than mercy towards the needy offered from the soul with pleasure and joy" - Maximus the Confessor, *Mystagogia, 24. PG. 91.713a.*

"We cannot be like God in essence, yet by progress in virtue we can imitate God. For that the Lord grants us the grace: be merciful as your heavenly Father is merciful" – Athanasius, *Ad Afros, 7.*

"Justice can wait, mercy cannot wait!" – Mother Teresa of Calcutta.

"Mercy: the ultimate and supreme act by which God comes to meet us. Mercy: the fundamental law that dwells in the heart of every person who looks sincerely into the eyes of his brothers and sisters on the path of life.

Mercy: the bridge that connects God and man, opening our hearts to a hope of being loved forever despite our sinfulness" – Pope Francis, *Misericordiae Vultus, 2.*

Meditation

I sit silent and relaxed. I try to become aware of the roles which I am forced to play in life. I accept myself as I have become, without judging or evoking guilt feelings. Slowly I begin to chant the name of Jesus with a mantra like Śree Yesu...Jai Yesu..Jai Jai Yesu OM...I feel the divine vibrations of compassion evolving in me. I recall the words of the Lord: "Be compassionate as your heavenly Father is compassionate." (Lk. 6:36).

Endnotes

[1] cit. Chariton, (1996), p. 164; Ware (1979), p. 71.

[2] cit. Chariton, (1996), p. 198.

[3] cit Ware (1979), p. 171.

[4] cit. Gillet (1987), p. 40.

[5] cit. *Writings from the Philokalia* (1995), p. 194.

[6] cit. *Writings from the Philokalia* (1995), p. 33.

[7] cit. Mello (1984) p. 277, 285.

[8] cit. Gillet (1987), p. 29.

[9] cit. Gillet (1987), p 40.

[10] cit. Chariton (1996), p. 114.

[11] cit. Gillet (1987), p. 37.

[12] *Way of a Pilgrim* (1978), p. 22.

[13] cit, Chariton (1996), p. 50.

[14] cit, Chariton (1996), p. 50.

[15] cit, Chariton (1996), p. 101.

[16] cit. Gillet (1987), p. 29.

[17] cit, Chariton (1996), p. 184.

[18] cit. Gillet (1987), p. 29.

[19] Ware (1979), p. 32.

[20] *Way of a Pilgrim* (1978) p. 34.

[21] Gillet (1987) p. 98.

[22] cit. Gillet (1987) p. 37.

[23] *Way of a Pilgrim* (1978), p. 40-41.

[24] cit. Gillet (1987). p. 28.

[25] cit. *Writings from the Philokalia* (1995), p.193.

[26] cit. Gillet (1987), p. 103.

[27] cit. Chariton (1996), p. 151.

[28] cit. Gillet (1987), p. 40.

[29] cit. Ware (1979), p. 88.

[30] cit. Ware (1979) p. 29.

[31] cit. Ware (1979) p. 162.

Bibliography

Canilang, Samuel Hermogeno, CMF (2010). *The Way of the Heart, Gregory Palamas and the Great Spiritual Traditions of Asia, The Encounter´s Relevance to Asian Religious Life*, Claretian Publications, Quezon City

Canilang, Samuel Hermogeno CMF (2012). *Gregory Palamas´s Theo-Anthropology and Mysticism according to Philakolia. Their Relevance to Religious Life in Asia*, Claretian Publications, Quezon City.

Catechism of the Catholic Church (1994). Theological Publications in India, Bangalore.

Chariton, Igumen, (1996). *The Art of Prayer*, Transl. E. Kadloubovsky and G.E.H. Palmer, Faber & Faber, New York.

Douglas-Klotz, Neil (1990). *Prayers of the Cosmos, Meditations on the Aramaic Words of Jesus*, Harper, San Francisco.

Gillet, Lev (1987). *The Jesus Prayer*, St. Vladimir Seminary, New York.

Griffiths, Bede (1982). *Marriage of East and West*, Collins, London.

Hausherr, Irene´ (1960). *Noms du Christ et voies d´oraison*, Pontificio Instituto Orientale, Rome.

Jalics, Franz SJ (1999). *Called to Share in his Life, Introduction to a Contemplative Way of Life and the Jesus Prayer*, transl. by L. Wiedenhöver, St Pauls, Bombay.

Jungclaussen, Emmanuel (2013). *Unterweisung im Herzensgebet*, EOS, St. Ottilien.

Köster, Peter SJ (2007). *Die Übung des Herzensgebetes nach der Tradition der Ostkirchen*, EOS Verlag, St. Ottilien.

Maloney, George SJ (2008). *Prayer of the Heart, The Contemplative Tradition of the Christian East*, Ave Maria Press, Notre dame.

Maschwitz, Rüdiger (2005). Das Herzensgebet, Ein Meditationsweg, Kösel, München.

Massa, Willi (ed) (1982). *Die Höhle des Herzens, Mantra-Praxis und Namensgebet*, Butzon & Bercker, Kevelaer.

Mello, Anthony de (1984). *Wellsprings, A Book of Spiritual Exercises*, GSP, Anand, India.

Mieth, Dietmar (1986). *Meister Eckhart, Einheit im Sein und Wirken*, Piper, München.

Monk of the Eastern Church (1967). *The Prayer of Jesus, Its Genesis, Development and Practice in the Byzantine-Slavic Religious Tradition*, Desclee, New York.

Mönch der Ostkirche (2001). Das *Jesusgebet, Anleitung zur Anrufung des Namens Jesu*, Edited by E. Jungclaussen, Friedrich Pustet, Regensburg.

Moses, Korko SJ (2014). *Jesu Nama Japam, The Practice of Jesus Prayer,* Claretians, Chennai.

Nataraja, Kim (2012). *Journey to the Heart, Christian Contemplation through the centuries,* Orbis, New York.

Painadath, Sebastian SJ (2009). *The Power of Silence, Fifty Meditations to Discover the Divine Space within you,* ISPCK, Delhi.

Painadath, Sebastian SJ (2014). *Spiritual Co-pilgrims, Towards a Christian Spirituality in Dialogue with Asian Religions,* ISPCK, Delhi.

Painadath, Sebastian SJ (2016). *Erkenne deine göttliche Natur, 55 Meditationen,* Vier-Türme Verlag, Münsterschwarzach.

Painadath, Sebastian SJ (2018). *You are divine, 100 Meditations on Theosis,* ISPCK, Delhi.

Painadath, Sebastian SJ / Rose Pudukadan (2014). *Das Herz in Schwingung bringen, Jesus-Gebet mit Mantras und Melodien,* Vier-Türme-Verlag, Münsterschwarach.

Palamas, Gregory (1983). *The Triads,* Translated by Nicholas Gendle, Paulist Press, New York.

Philokalia (2009). English and Malayalam translations, 5 volumes, published by Cherian Eapen, Roy International Children´s Foundation, 5 b, Century Towers, Kottayam, India.

Pieris, Alois SJ, (1989). *Love Meets Wisdom,* Orbis, New York.

Punnapadam, Thomas SDB (2005) *The Jesus Prayer, A Rediscovery,* Christujyoti, Bangalore.

Rohr, Richard (2016). *The Divine Dance, The Trinity and your Transformation,* SPCK, London.

Ruhbach, Gerhard / Josef Sudbrack SJ (1989). *Christliche Mystik, Texte aus zwei Jahrtausenden,* CH Beck, Munich.

Sjogren, Per-Olof (1996). *The Jesus Prayer,* SPCK, London.

Sorsky, Nil (2003). *Complete Writings,* Translated by George A. Maloney SJ, Paulist Press, New York.

Ware, Kallistos (1979). *The Orthodox Way,* Mowbray, London.

Way of a Pilgrim (1978). Translated by Helen Bacovcin, Image Books, Doubleday, New York.

Writings from the Philokalia (1995). Translation of Passij Velickowskij´s Russian book *Dobrotolubie by* E. Kadloubovsky and G.E.H. Palmer, Faber & Faber, New York.

www.ingramcontent.com/pod-product-compliance
Lightning Source LLC
Chambersburg PA
CBHW030334020726
47493CB00004B/1274